TAKE
TWO

ALSO BY JULIA DeVILLERS
AND JENNIFER ROY

TRADING FACES

TaKe TWO

Julia DeVillers
Jennifer Roy

ALADDIN
NEW YORK   LONDON   TORONTO   SYDNEY

ALADDIN
An imprint of Simon & Schuster Children's Publishing Division
1230 Avenue of the Americas, New York, NY 10020
First Aladdin hardcover edition January 2010
Copyright © 2010 by Julia DeVillers and Jennifer Roy
All rights reserved, including the right of reproduction
in whole or in part in any form.
ALADDIN is a trademark of Simon & Schuster, Inc.,
and related logo is a registered trademark of Simon & Schuster, Inc.
For information about special discounts for bulk purchases,
please contact Simon & Schuster Special Sales at 1-866-506-1949
or business@simonandschuster.com.
The Simon & Schuster Speakers Bureau can bring authors to
your live event. For more information or to book an event contact
the Simon & Schuster Speakers Bureau at 1-866-248-3049
or visit our website at www.simonspeakers.com.
Designed by Karin Paprocki
The text of this book was set in Granjon.
Manufactured in the United States of America
1109 MTN
2 4 6 8 10 9 7 5 3 1
Library of Congress Cataloging-in-Publication Data
DeVillers, Julia.
Take two / by Julia DeVillers and Jennifer Roy.
— 1st Aladdin hardcover ed.
p. cm.
Summary: Identical twins Payton and Emma continue
to navigate life in middle school as they serve their punishment
for having fooled people by trading places, and they learn
that their own identities are usually best.
ISBN: 978-1-4169-7533-5 (hardcover edition)
[1. Twins—Fiction. 2. Sisters—Fiction. 3. Individuality—Fiction.
4. Middle schools—Fiction. 5. Schools—Fiction.]
I. Roy, Jennifer Rozines, 1967– II. Title.
PZ7.D4974Tak 2010
[Fic]—dc22
2009038222

To Robin Rozines (Mom)

TAKE TWO

One

MIDDLE SCHOOL AFTER LAST PERIOD

Cell phone! Oh, no, my cell phone was ringing!

I opened my tote bag and scrounged around in a panic. I felt my brush and mirror. My raspberry lip gloss. Ouch, sharp pencil.

And phew, my cell phone. I changed the ringer to vibrate. And not a moment too soon because the principal was walking toward us . . . toward us . . . and, whew. She walked right by us.

My phone went *bzzzzt*.

"Good job, Payton," my twin sister, Emma, muttered. "Aren't we in enough trouble without you breaking the no-cell-phones-on-during-school rule, too?"

Why yes. Yes, we were in enough trouble. Considering we were on our way to after-school *detention*.

"Plus, we are only allowed to use our cell phones for emergencies. We're already grounded. We don't need to get in any more trouble." Emma went on and on and on . . .

I sighed as I walked down the hall. We passed a WELCOME, GECKOS! poster that was peeling off the wall. Someone had drawn a mustache and earrings on the gecko, the school mascot.

Only a little more than a week ago, I'd been so psyched to be at this new school. My own locker! New people! Cute guys! Different teachers! Switching classes!

But then, we had switched more than classes. We had switched places. And the whole identical twins trading places thing? Hadn't worked out so well for us.

We passed two boys walking the other way. One turned around and laughed.

"Hey, look!" he said. "It's those TV twins!"

They both laughed.

My face flamed red with embarrassment. The whole weekend I'd tried to prepare myself for that kind of comment. It had been a seriously long day.

"I wonder if they know who is who today," his friend called out loudly, obviously so we could hear him.

"Who is *whom*," Emma muttered as she walked next to me, lugging her ginormous backpack.

I rolled my eyes at her.

"What?" Emma said. "If they're going to be insulting, they could at least be grammatically correct."

And then she turned around to call to the boys.

"It's whom! W-H-O-M!"

"Oh my gosh," I said, grabbing her backpack strap and dragging her around the corner. "Shush!"

❀ 2 ❀

"But he was being inaccurate," she protested. "And he was trying to make us look silly, but I showed him, didn't I? Ha! Did you see the look of embarrassment on his face after I pointed out his error?"

Augh! He wasn't embarrassed about his grammar, he was embarrassed for my sister. Emma was so entirely clueless sometimes.

"Just let it go," I moaned. "Isn't it bad enough that we're known as the identical twins who switched places, fooled everyone until they were busted, and were filmed making complete idiots of themselves in front of the entire school last week?"

"'Who' is a subjective pronoun," Emma muttered. "Duh."

Sigh.

Even though last week was only our first week in our new school, we were already kind of famous. But not in a good way. Being called the "TV twins" sounded cool, until you knew the whole story. We hadn't been on real TV, just the school video-cast shown live on a humongous screen at our first pep rally. When, unknown to us at the time, we were on camera arguing about Emma being a boring brainiac. And about me not doing so great at hanging out with popular people. Basically, in front of our entire school, we had a fight and called each other super-ficial, shallow, selfish, dumb and . . . Let's just say we totally embarrassed ourselves.

"I wish we could start middle school over again," I said. "We need a do-over."

"Tell me about it," Emma agreed. "I'm going to detention.

Me! Emma 'The Brain' Mills! I've only stayed after for math-letes, a spelling bee, or to help the sixth-grade math teacher understand our honors homework. But detention?"

"It was *your* idea to switch places," I reminded her.

"Because *you* needed me to help save your reputation after you embarrassed yourself in front of your so-called friends," Emma shot back. "And look where that got us. Right into the principal's office *and* detention *and* being grounded."

Ugh. My sister was right. It seemed like a good idea at the time, switching places. Emma and I looked so much alike, we'd thought we could get away with it—and that it would be a minor break from our normal lives, which hadn't been going so great.

"Detention! I think I'm going to hyperventilate. No, worse, I'm going to pass out," Emma was muttering while unzipping her hoodie.

"Emma! Your sweatshirt!" I whispered, trying not to attract any more attention from people passing by.

"What? All this stress is making me hot," Emma said, starting to pull off her sweatshirt.

"Emma, look at what you're wearing," I said, tilting my head toward her T-shirt so she'd get the picture. It said BEE THE BEST SPELLER IN SIXTH GRADE! It was bright yellow and had a freakish-looking bee wearing a crown on its head. She'd worn that thing all last year and it still made my eyes bleed.

With Emma's newfound sort-of sense of style, I knew even *she* would be embarrassed by it. I smiled at the thought of

Emma having even a small sense of style. Up until last week, Emma's idea of style was to throw on sweats, tie her hair up in a ponytail, and wear a T-shirt from one of her gajillion competitions, advertising her brilliance. Even for the first day of school!

But I'd wanted to start the school year looking trendy and cool. So I'd spent the summer in camp doing chores for this girl, Ashlynn, who would pay me in her designer clothes. I called them my "Summer Slave clothes."

The designer clothes had impressed this popular girl Sydney and given me temporary access to popularity. But very temporary, because then I'd totally embarrassed myself. Emma had stepped in to save me and we'd switched places. She helped me redeem myself with Sydney and her friends.

It worked for a couple days and then? Twin Fail.

But one good thing? Emma had discovered that looking comfortable and cute wasn't such a bad thing. I waited as she opened her mouth to thank me for saving her from being seen in that T-shirt in public.

"Please tell me you're not concerned with what I'm wearing right now or how I look?" Emma hissed at me.

Well, I was. Kind of. Her hair was really disastrous, since taking off the sweatshirt had caused a static attack. I reached into my tote bag and scrounged around. Mirror, lip gloss, ouch! Sharp pencil. Yeesh. And then there it was, my brush.

"That is the least of our problems right now," Emma said. "I can't believe you are even thinking about my appearance!"

I quickly dropped the brush back into the tote bag.

"Besides, this is the perfect shirt to wear," Emma muttered. "It will remind Mrs. Case that I am the Spelling Bee Champion and not someone who gets in Big Trouble."

Well, at least it would be harder to mix us up, with Emma's static-head and goofy T-shirt. My hair was still looking good even after a bad day. My brownish blond, shiny hair was my best feature. Emma also had brownish blond hair, but it was a teeny bit less shiny than mine.

And I was pleased with my outfit today. I'd spent a lot of time choosing it. Since it was our first day back after our horrible humiliation, I wanted to make sure that when people pointed and stared at me at least I looked cute.

I was wearing:

☑ A blue long-sleeved shirt
(Summer Slave clothes)

☑ A lighter blue tank
(From when Emma had gone on a shopping spree for me)

☑ Jeans
(Summer Slave)

☑ Bracelet with the *P* on it
(Mine)

☑ Sneakers
(Mine. I was done wearing Ashlynn's too-big shoes with their too-high heels.)

I noticed my sneaker was untied. Oh, shoot. That's all I would need, to embarrass myself by tripping over my shoelace. I bent down to tie it, and didn't notice someone rounding the corner until a white sneaker practically kicked me in the head.

"Hey!" I yelped. And looked up into the face of Sydney.

"Oh, it's just the twins," Sydney said dismissively, looking down at me and then at Emma.

Ugh. It's The Sydney. She was wearing a green-and-yellow Geckos cheerleading uniform and holding pom-poms that were at my eye level. She obviously noticed that, too, and shook them so they swatted me in the face. I stood up quickly and stepped back.

"I can't believe you twins!" Following Sydney, as always, was her friend Cashmere. "You guys could have injured Sydney, and that would be a disaster. Sydney is going to *cheer-leading practice*."

Sydney was cheerleading? Since when?

"Didn't you hear?" Cashmere asked after seeing the look on my face. "Sydney's on cheer squad! Daphne Yee broke her ankle, and Serra Potter moved to California. Sydney was the second alternate! Everyone knows she should have made it in the first place."

"Oh, Cashmere." Sydney giggled and faked a modest smile. "Let's go. Can't be late for cheerleading practice!"

Sydney did a *Rah!* move with her arms. I could hear Cashmere's voice as they sauntered down the hall. "Did you see Twin #2's outfit? It was sooo cute. I *so* want those jeans."

"Shut it, Cashmere," Sydney growled, and they walked on down the hall.

"Ugh, I *don't* appreciate being called Twin #2. Cashmere and Sydney obviously know my name is Payton," I grumbled. Sydney and Cashmere had ignored me completely all day. Well, except for giggling and whispering about me.

"Of course they do, because they were your FBFs," Emma said cheerfully.

"BFFs," I said, glaring at her. "How come you can win spelling bees but you can't remember three letters in a row? And speaking of, can you please cover up that hideous shirt?"

Not that I cared what Sydney thought about Emma's style anymore. Of course I didn't. Not even a little bit.

"This shirt is more rare than one of your designer fashions," Emma said pointedly. "Not everyone can win a spelling bee."

And then she stopped walking. And pointed to a door that said DETENTION.

Emma started to hyperventilate. Loudly.

"I can't! I can't go in a detention room!" Emma gasped. "Won't somebody stop this madness!?"

She was totally having a panic attack!

"Emma!" I pushed her toward the door. "Chill out! Do your breathing thing!"

Emma always did some breathing relaxation thing before her big competitions. It helped calm her down. I'd see her pacing the halls before the spelling bee or whatever we're-smarter-than-you genius contest she was in.

"Relaxing, cleansing breaths," she muttered. "In through the nose. Out through the mouth. Slow, deep breaths."

She closed her eyes and started breathing slowly and deeply. And loudly.

"Nose in, mouth out," I coached her.

"There are those twins," a girl's voice said. "Oh my gosh, are they talking to each other in a secret twin language?"

I looked in the detention room to see two girls staring at Emma and me in fascination.

"Yeah, I heard twins talk to each other in their own language, but I've never seen it before," another girl's voice said. "Spooky."

"We're breathing, okay?" I snapped. "Even twins breathe! Yeesh!"

The girls looked startled.

"We have to go in there," I said to Emma gently. "Just take a little baby step and—"

Emma whimpered.

"Excuse me!" A boy was walking quickly down the hall toward us. "Are you Payton and Emma Mills?"

"Yes." I sighed. "Yes, we're the identical embarrassing twins from TV. Yes, we switched places and it didn't go well. Yes, my hair is lighter and Emma's a little taller."

"Uh . . ." The boy looked slightly confused. "I just have a message to give you from the guidance counselor."

Oh. I took the note and read it aloud. "'You are excused from detention today. Please go to the guidance office.' Signed, Counselor Case."

"Follow me," the boy said.

Emma's eyes lit up as she backed away from the detention room.

"Excuse me, you know what this is about?" I asked the boy.

"I don't know." He shrugged. "All I know is that Counselor Case was complaining about troublemaker twins and they are going to be in So. Much. Trouble."

Emma and I looked at each other and gulped. We walked in silence down the hall, not looking at each other the entire way, and into the guidance office.

A dark-haired woman was sitting behind a desk. When she saw us, she stood up and gestured for us to take a seat.

"I'm Counselor Case," she said. "Please sit down."

Emma and I sat down. We gave each other a worried look.

"I'm afraid this is a sticky situation," the counselor said. "Twin issues are challenging. It must be hard to be identical twins and feel constantly compared to each other. You must feel like you have to stand out to have your own identity. And sometimes, that can lead to trouble. Big trouble."

And then she got up suddenly and left the room.

Emma

Two

GUIDANCE OFFICE

Trouble: (noun or verb)
A source of difficulty.
Synonyms: concern, upset, suffering

I tried to soothe my panic with dictionary definitions I'd memorized last summer for fun. And so I wouldn't think about what was happening to me.

Up until last week, the words "trouble" and "Emma" were never remotely related to each other. I never got in trouble in school. I never even had trouble *with* school. School came very naturally to me. Unlike Payton, my not-as-smart twin.

"What do you think she meant?" Payton whispered to me.

I took a deep breath and let my intellect take over my emotions. Just like I did in final-round academic competitions where there was no room for nervousness.

"Well, she said that twin issues are challenging," I said.

"And she is correct in that forming separate identities can sometimes lead to extreme behavior in order to prove there's a difference."

"I meant, what do you think she means by 'big trouble'?" Payton interrupted me. "Do you think she means more trouble than detention? Like, suspension?"

Gasp! I hadn't thought of that.

"Or since it's the guidance office, maybe they're going to tell us that this is going to go on our college records?" Payton continued.

My throat made kind of a strangled noise and I put my head in my hands. Now I felt like I was really going to pass out.

Suddenly we heard a voice approaching.

"And I mean BIG trouble." It was Counselor Case, and she walked in through the open door.

Payton and I both started talking at once.

"We didn't mean to cause big trouble," my twin said.

"We're really not troublemakers," I wailed. I started to hyperventilate again. Clearly, my brain could not save me this time.

"Girls! Girls! I think there's a misunderstanding," Counselor Case said. "I wasn't referring to you."

What? I looked up.

Two boys walked into the room and stood near her desk. They looked like they were about eight, with reddish hair. They were both wearing light blue Polo shirts and khaki-and-blue plaid shorts.

Payton and I gave each other a knowing look. They were definitely identical twins.

"The identical twins who are in big trouble are these two boys here." Counselor Case sighed. "This is Mason next to me, and that's Jason."

"Hi," the boys both said politely.

"Hi, Mason," Payton said, carefully looking at the right one. "Hi, Jason."

Ooh, my sister was clever, showing the boys that she cared enough not to mix them up. I, on the other hand, said nothing. Little kids and me? Not on the same wavelength.

"These are my twin sons," Counselor Case explained. "They're having a few identical twin challenges of their own. And while I know you're supposed to be in detention, I thought perhaps you might want some school service instead."

"Mason's tutor quit," Jason said. "And our mom heard *one* of you was really smart."

That would be me.

"Jason!" Counselor Case stammered. "Both of them are very smart. Of course, all children have their talents and gifts as well as their learning challenges. But Emma and Payton, how would you feel about being reassigned from detention to provide a school service?"

"Great!" Payton and I both said. Obviously.

"Let's say . . ." Counselor Case looked at us. "Just randomly . . . Emma, you can tutor Mason in math."

Random would mean that there was an equal probability of Payton and me being chosen. Ha, she wasn't being random at all. Statistically I was one hundred percent the math choice. Statistics was one of my passions. I smiled just thinking about it.

"And Payton, you can babysit Jason," the counselor said.

"Wait!" Jason said. "How come I don't get a math tutor?"

"Erm," Counselor Case said, and lowered her voice. "Honey, you don't need a math tutor."

"But that's not fair if he gets a tutor and I only get a babysitter," Jason said. "I want a math tutor."

"Well, okay, I can tutor math," Payton offered. "What are you learning? Adding? Subtracting?"

"Can you tutor me in algebra?" he asked her.

I choked, covering it up with a fake coughing fit. Algebra is taught in eighth or ninth grade and Payton is only in seventh-grade math. Barely.

"Jason is slightly advanced for his age in math," Counselor Case said. "Mason needs the math help—"

Ah. Mason = the nongenius twin. Jason = the genius twin. Got it.

"To be honest I was also hoping to transfer Emma's joy for math to Mason as well," Counselor Case said. "Do you have joy for math, Payton?"

I snorted. Payton kicked me.

"Why am I being punished?" Jason whined. "I want a math tutor, too," he said again.

"Well, Jason," Payton said in a talking-to-little-kids voice. "If you want a tutor, you know who is really good at math?"

"Pythagoras?" Jason replied.

"No, I meant Emma!" Payton said. "Emma could tutor you, too, and spread her joy for math to both of you."

I shot her a look. Payton smiled smugly at me.

"Fine, Jason, you also can be tutored by Emma," Counselor Case said, looking a little weary. "We'll set up a week-by-week schedule for Emma and both boys."

"I'll put it in my planner," I said.

Counselor Case turned around and started entering the dates on her wall calendar. And when she wasn't watching, the twins started going at it.

I watched Mason poke Jason. Jason kicked him back. Mason balled his hands into a fist and—

"Boys!" I said sharply. Whew! That startled them. "Bring your notebooks, math textbooks, and freshly sharpened pencils."

There. I sounded professionally tutorlike. I was confident about the math. It was the Mason/Jason part that somewhat freaked me out. And what about Payton? Was she going to have to go to detention, after all?

I looked over at Payton. She looked nervous.

"Payton, we need to find a suitable activity for you," Counselor Case said, flipping through a binder on her desk. "Football, no. Do you speak German? No? Hmm, Drama Club is starting. . . ."

"I could join Drama Club," Payton offered.

Hey! Payton already had wanted to join Drama Club, but she couldn't because of detention. Wasn't she supposed to be punished? Why was I going to be stuck with these small creatures while she got what she'd wanted?

"Drama Club is an excellent idea, Payton," she said. "We'll set up a schedule for you, too. I'm just going to drop off some paperwork and I'll be right back."

Counselor Case stood up and walked out of the room.

Payton, the boys, and I sat there and looked at each other. And then one of them talked.

"Are you two identical?" Jason asked.

"Yeah," I said. "Just like you guys."

"No, you look different. *Her* nose is fatter than hers," Mason said, pointing first to Payton, then to me. "But the other one's fingers are stubbier."

"Mason!" I exclaimed. "You guys of all people should know how awkward it is to have people compare you with your twin."

"Duh," Mason said. "They're always like, 'Mason, how come you have such a doofus for a twin?'"

"*I'm* the doofus? You're so dumb the last tutor quit because she couldn't teach you," Jason retorted.

Mason jumped up, fist clenched.

"Guys!" Payton said. "GUYS! Enough! Stop picking on each other. Be nice!"

The boys sat down. Good job, Payton. The boys were

silent. Then Mason turned to his brother and broke the silence.

"Doesn't it weird you out that her left eye is bigger?" he asked. "But the other one's right eye is bigger?"

"It is?" Payton and I each clutched one eye.

"Look, her eye twitches when she's freaked." Mason laughed. "And that one chews her hair."

Payton clutched her other eye as I dropped my piece of hair.

The door opened again and Counselor Case walked back in.

"Did you have a chance for twin bonding?" She smiled at all of us. "You identical twins always have those special twin stories that the rest of us can't understand."

"Oh, we're bonding." I gave a sickly little smile. Bonding like two electrons with a negative charge. Which, as everyone knows, repel each other.

I had to keep up a happy appearance, however. Because not only did a counselor have the power to get me out of detention, I realized something else. As my guidance counselor, she would be guiding my middle school career—recommending me for enrichment classes and academic camps and all of the stuff that would go on my record for college.

Counselor Case held my entire future in her hands. I glanced down at my lucky shirt to remind me of my strength in pressure situations.

"Jason and Mason?" I said.

The boys eyed me suspiciously.

"Did you know that Payton's and my age squared minus your age squared equals ten times your age?"

Counselor Case smiled. Payton rolled her eyes. Mason groaned loudly.

"Duh," Jason said.

"Well, I think we are in business," said Counselor Case. "Boys, say good-bye to Payton and Emma."

"Good-bye, Pain-ton and Elmo," one of the boys said as the other one laughed.

We got out of there. Fast. As we headed down the hallway we could hear the counselor saying something to the boys. She did not sound happy.

"Payton," I said. "I'm going to be tutoring the monster twins. Whose mother holds the key to my college future in her hands."

"Oh, yeah. I guess you can't mess up or it will really screw things up for you," Payton said cheerfully.

I glared at her. She didn't seem too sympathetic.

"You're thinking about how you get to go to Drama Club instead, aren't you?" I accused her. People always wondered if twins could read each other's mind, but it didn't take a genius to figure that one out.

"No," Payton said. "Okay, yes. And I was also thinking about how for once it's good that I stink at math, so I don't have to tutor those boys."

"I'm doomed," I moaned as we neared our lockers. "I know zero about boys."

"I've noticed," Payton said. "But you're about to get some practice."

What? Oh. Whoa.

Walking down the hall toward us was Ox.

"Hey, Emma," he said. "Hey, Payton."

"Oh . . . ahhh . . . h-hi," I stuttered. Pull yourself together, Emma. "Well, hello, Ox."

That didn't sound much better.

"Hi, Ox," Payton said, not sounding like a stammering idiot.

"I'm done with practice," Ox said. "Are you guys going to the bus? I'm heading over there."

I looked at Ox, in his blue button-down shirt and jeans. I quickly looked at my watch. There was still ten minutes left until the late bus dismissal. I shot a look at Payton.

"Emma is," Payton said. "And I was just heading to the snack machines, so I'll see you on the bus, Emma. Bye, Ox!"

She left.

So, it was me and Ox. Ox and me. The football player I'd gotten to know during our twin-switching. Even though Ox had originally thought I was Payton, it turned out he liked me—the *real* me. Emma.

But I still wasn't sure if he *like* liked me. At least, like I *like* liked him. I mean, just because he happened to be walking down the hall doesn't mean . . . He was just being polite by stopping to chat, right? Right? Did he just happen to be here? Oh, this is confusing. It was still hard to believe I had a crush on someone named *Ox*, which sounds like a big, dumb jock, but only the jock part is true. Payton told me the team quarterback has to be pretty smart to remember the plays.

"Emma, I—," Ox started to say.

I turned to look at him. Boy, was he cute. His hair was all rumpled from practice and he was so muscley and—

Clannnng! Clannnng! The late-dismissal bell went off.

Ox's lips were moving, but I couldn't hear what he was saying.

The bell stopped. There was an awkward silence. What? What had he been saying?

Emma, I was wondering if you want to go out with me? . . . Emma, do you think Sydney would go out with me? . . . Emma, I . . . What?!?!?!

"Hang on, I have a text," Ox said, pulling out a black cell. "Oh, my mom's picking me up instead. She's out front. So, I better go."

Ox was leaving! I had to say something!

"Ox!" I blurted out. Um. "Ox! Did you know there's a Festival of the Ox in Brazil? It attracts tens of thousands of visitors every year."

Oh. My. Gosh. Why did I have to blurt out geek trivia whenever I panicked? I felt my face—no, my whole self— turn red with embarrassment.

"You know about the Boi Bumba festival?" Ox asked. "I'm planning to go there to celebrate when I get older."

"Well, it is a celebration of you," I agreed.

We smiled at each other.

"And *boi* is the Portuguese word for 'ox,'" I continued, encouraged. "Which is appropriate because, well, you're a boy. So you could be a boy *boi*. I mean, a girl *boi* would be weird, right? Ha! A girl *boi*!"

Ox's smile faltered a bit.

Speaking of weird . . . I willed myself to just shut up.

"I better go," he said, and waved.

Bye. *Boi*.

I slunk away in the opposite direction, toward the late bus. First, twin boy troublemakers. And now Boi Bumba babbling. Sigh. Why couldn't boys be as simple as math?

Three

AFTER SCHOOL

"Give me an *M*!" Emma said to me.

I gave her a look. We were both at our lockers putting away our stuff and getting ready for our after-school activities. Emma had mathletes starting in a half hour, and she was heading to the library to wait until it started.

"Give me an *A*!" she persisted. "Give me a *T* and a *H*! Go, mathletes!"

"Emma, shush," I said. "Haven't we had enough people staring at us today? Besides, mathletes don't have cheerleaders."

"Mathletes have everything," Emma said, putting her usual six thousand tons of books into her backpack. "We have intelligence, enthusiasm, and new scientific calculators. Woohoo!"

She punched the air awkwardly. Sydney had no worries

about Emma joining cheerleading, that was for sure.

"Hey, are you those two twins from TV?" some boy passing us asked.

"No," I replied. "Today, we are not even remotely related."

I slammed my locker shut.

"Payton," Emma said. "I'm sorry if my enthusiasm for academics embarrasses you. Things have been such a downer lately, I just lost myself in a rare moment of happiness. I didn't mean to embarrass you."

Oh. I felt really bad.

"It's okay," I said guiltily.

"Hah! Tricked you! My master manipulation skills are ready to take on that Jazmine James," Emma said. Now she not only punched the air, but she did an awkward jump. "Mathletes rock! Goooo, mathletes!"

Augh. Sometimes, she just had no shame.

"Goooo, Emma." I sighed. Please, just go, so people will stop looking at us.

Emma waved good-bye and left, to my relief. However, I did kind of understand why she was so excited. Not because of doing math, of course. But because I was excited to go to Drama. From detention to Drama Club! Here's the thing. Last week when I was pretending to be Emma, I'd gotten to go live on air for our school's first videocast. And I'd loved it. So being onstage seemed like something I might like, too.

Not that I thought I was going to get a big part in a play or anything, of course. But it would be cool to get a small role and have a couple lines to say. Emma could be the Mathletes Twin, I could be the Actress Twin!

I smiled at the thought of it.

And then my cell phone started buzzing. I saw a text was coming from Tess. She'd texted me a couple times, even though she was one of Jazmine James's sidekicks. Emma called Jazmine her "archnemesis," but even she agreed Tess seemed kind of nice.

i m walking in2 drama! i m saving u a seat!

I smiled and shut my locker. I walked down the hall to the auditorium, feeling more confident since I knew I had a seat saved for me. I walked into the auditorium and saw that the front rows were filled with people facing the darkened stage.

I scanned the room, looking for Tess. I spotted Nick. I was a little surprised he wasn't at mathletes, since he was a math brain. But since he was the camera guy for VOGS (Videocast of Gecko Students), I guess it wasn't too surprising he would be at drama.

He saw me, too, and waved. Nick was so nice and easy to talk to that even Emma had been able to talk to him. I'd once thought they would be the perfect love match. He looked kind of her brainiac type, with a little messy longish brown hair and green eyes. But then Emma had totally surprised me—and everyone else—by liking Ox.

I looked around some more and saw Tess. Tess was pretty easy to spot since she was seriously tall with long blond hair. She was sitting in the middle of second row, so I made my way over there.

"Excuse me," I said to the person sitting on the end as I climbed over her legs. "Excuse me."

And then someone didn't excuse me, and I tripped over her legs.

"Owww," she whined dramatically.

It was Sydney. And she was so obviously intentionally blocking the aisle.

"I didn't see you," she said innocently. "Besides, aren't you supposed to be in detention?"

"Aren't you supposed to be in cheerleading?" I asked back.

"I'm doing it all," she said, smiling. "Preparing for my future career as actress/model/professional cheerleader."

"Whatever," I muttered, and backed away, down the aisle where I'd come from. I'd just go around to the other side of the row. I was looking for Drama, but not *girl* drama.

"Sydney, you're so talented," I heard a girl say.

I inched back over everyone's legs, just as the lights went on.

A teacher came out onto the stage. "Welcome, students!"

It was Mrs. Burkle! Our English teacher, who also ran VOGS.

"People! Be seated!"

I stepped over the last leg and into the aisle and then

sneaked up the aisle to get to the front and back over to Tess's chair.

"I'll begin with a quote from Shakespeare!" Burkle said. "'To be or not to be'! As in, to be or not to be seated is your choice! But if you are not in a chair, you will be excused from the room!"

I slid into a chair next to Tess. Whew!

"We'll put on some fabulous shows on this very stage. We will waste no time! We will begin auditions for our first play this very week!"

There was an excited murmur. I happily pictured myself in costume and performing to cheers and applause.

"Mrs. Burkle, what play will we be doing?" some boy asked.

"Our first play will be . . ." Mrs. Burkle paused. *"The Wizard of Oz."*

Oh! I love that movie! Except The Flying Monkeys kind of freaked me out. But I'd even play a Flying Monkey if I could be in this play. Or a Munchkin, I'd even play a Munchkin. I'd pretty much play any part.

"Mrs. Burkle?"

"Somebody's voice projects nice and clear." Mrs. Burkle smiled broadly. "I like that. What is your name?"

"Sydney Fish," Sydney said, nicely and clearly. "I have a question. I love *Wizard of Oz* and I want to be an actress. But I have a previous commitment because I am a cheerleader. May I still audition?"

"Certain roles will take a major commitment," Mrs. Burkle said. "Such as Dorothy. However, there are other roles in fewer scenes that might fit into a busy after-school schedule."

Hmm. That would be excellent if Sydney had to be a Flying Monkey or a Munchkin. He-he.

"Like Glinda, the glamourous Good Witch of the North?" Sydney asked.

"Exactly," Mrs. Burkle said.

I silently groaned. That was practically a done deal, because Sydney pretty much got whatever she wanted. Except for one thing. Well, one person, anyway . . .

Sydney didn't get Ox. Sydney had flirted with Ox, but somehow he ended up liking my sister. I still couldn't get over the fact that not only did my sister have a boy she liked like her back, but one that Sydney wanted. Sometimes, things just didn't make sense.

"Who do you want to be?" Tess whispered to me. "I hope we don't want the same role."

"That's nice of you to ask," I whispered back. "But I've never done a play before so I'll be happy to be a Munchkin. How about you?"

"Oh, anything." She shrugged. "But I doubt I'll be a Munchkin."

We both grinned. Tess towered over most of us, including the boys.

"Let's start by doing a few warm-up exercises my favorite drama coach taught me," Mrs. Burkle announced. "Stand up and choose a partner. Find a space with your partner onstage or in the aisle."

"Partner?" Tess asked me.

And we got up and moved out to the aisle to find a space. I noticed Sydney hopped up onto the front of the stage.

"This exercise is called 'Mirror Image,'" Mrs. Burkle said. "Face your partner. One student will act as leader, the other follower. The leader will mime actions while the follower will try to match anything done by the leader. Your goal is to be so synchronized that it's as if you are a reflection in a mirror."

"You can be the leader," I said, facing Tess.

Tess raised her hands over her head, and I raised mine to match.

"You should be really good at this game," Tess said as she moved slowly and I mimicked her. "Since it's called Mirror Image and you've got one in real life."

"True." I sighed. "Not that Emma and I really are in synch most of the time. She's so different from me."

Tess made a goofy face and I imitated it, trying not to laugh. Then Tess did a more complicated hand motion.

"Excellent!" The voice behind me made me jump. "Here is a team that is demonstrating a near-perfect mirror image! Everyone please watch."

Oh my gosh! She was talking to Tess and me!

We did our mirror image, and I tried to ignore the fact that everyone was watching us do it.

"Fabulous!" Mrs. Burkle said.

She said I was wonderful! This was awesome! It was like I'd already had a preaudition for her or something. I turned around and grinned.

"Oh! Ms. Mills! I did not recognize you from the back," Mrs. Burkle said.

I felt a little like a celebrity.

"I didn't realize you were here," she said. "Please head up to the stage to see Zahra in the red shirt. Zahra is our high school intern here to assist."

Okay! I looked at Tess and she shrugged at me. I felt a little bad leaving her, and getting all that attention out in front of everyone. I practically skipped up the stage steps. I was sooo glad I'd joined Drama. It was going better than I'd imagined! I passed Sydney on the stage and gave her a sweet smile. Ha! Take that, Sydney!

"Hi, I'm Payton," I said to Zahra.

"Follow me," Zahra said.

"Um, okay."

I followed her off to the side of the stage and out the side door. Then she reached down on the floor and pulled up a handle. A trapdoor opened up and her head went down, down, down, as if she were climbing down a ladder.

"Excuse me, where did you go?" I leaned carefully over the opening in the floor. I saw a short ladder leading to the floor.

"To the basement room," she called up. "Come on down."

Um, huh? As I leaned over a little farther and looked down, I saw a dusty room full of shelves with things like paint and I don't know what else on them. There was an old makeup-style table with a mirror on it, a rack with hangers. Theater things that looked like they hadn't been used since before Emma and I were born.

"Why do I need to come down?" I asked cautiously.

"I'll show you," she said.

I climbed down the ladder, rung by rung. I sneezed from the dustiness.

"You're here to do school service instead of detention or something, right?" Zahra asked. "We need you to clean and reorganize the stage basement. Mrs. Burkle wants to use it for a costume-slash-supply room to keep the sets in. There's a broom and dustpan in the corner. Let me know if you need anything!"

Zahra climbed back up the ladder. And I was alone. In the stage basement. Because of school service instead of detention. It suddenly dawned on me that I wasn't going to be part of Drama onstage. I was supposed to be cleaning under the stage.

Too bad we weren't doing *Cinderella*, I would have been perfect.

"Hello? Payton?" I heard a voice from above. Sydney's face appeared in the hole in the ceiling.

And if this were *Cinderella*, she would be a Wicked Stepsister.

"Hah! You're in, like, the dungeon! Gross!" Sydney laughed. "Mrs. Burkle said to give you this."

Suddenly a mop hovered through the opening, spraying dirt all over me.

"Ooopsie," Sydney said. "My bad."

She cackled. Forget Glinda. She would make an excellent Wicked Witch. I grabbed the mop from her, coughing.

"And here's the bucket," she said.

And as I looked up to catch a glimpse of a bucket. A bucket that tilted sideways and—

Water came splashing down on my head! Brown, smelly water!

"Ooopsie," Sydney said again. "My bad again."

"Sydney!" I tried to yell at her, but her head disappeared. I heard footsteps running away.

I was drenched in water that was apparently used to clean the floor, and from the smell of it, not recently. I caught a glimpse of myself in the reflection of the mirror. I was disgusting.

Bzzzzt! I limply pulled my phone out of my pocket. It was from Tess.

P: getting drama club pix 4 yrbk! & headshot
pix 2 use 4 audition. Come up!!!!!!!

I sank down on the bucket. This was all because of our stupid twin switching! This totally and completely stunk.

❀ 31 ❀

I blinked back tears and tried not to cry. Okay, that wasn't working. I pretty much started to cry.

I started to text Tess back that I wasn't coming. Just go on without me, Drama people. Don't mind me, covered in muddy water in the filthy basement.

Bzzzzt! It was Emma.

Do u have the starring role yet? Should I ask for ur autograph? lol.

Not particularly good timing for Emma's attempt at humor. I texted back.

No. Everything stinks. Including me.

Almost immediately, my phone buzzed with a call.

"So, I've got a few minutes to kill before mathletes. What stinks?" Emma asked me. Then she paused. "Are you crying? You're crying. Why are you crying? Tell me what happened."

I told Emma what happened.

"Oh," Emma said sympathetically. "That does stink."

"And *I* stink. I smell disgusting because I'm covered with muddy water while everyone else is going to get their picture taken," I concluded miserably. "I won't be in the yearbook picture. And I won't get a headshot."

"But you should have a headshot for your audition if everyone else does," Emma said indignantly.

"I can't audition," I said. "I'm on cleanup duty."

"But at least you have to be in the yearbook picture," Emma said. "You have to prove to everyone you're part of Drama Club, no matter what! What if Counselor Case sees the picture and thinks you skipped out on Drama Club? Your yearbook picture is proof."

"I guess she could ask Burkle if I was here—," I said, but Emma wasn't listening.

"Sydney cannot sabotage this, too!" Emma said. "Enough is enough. March up there and get your picture taken."

"Emma," I wailed. "I'm covered in muddy water! I'm a mess!"

There was silence at the end of the phone.

"Payton. Meet me at the JC. Now."

And I heard the click of Emma hanging up the phone.

The JC? The JC was the janitor's closet, our secret twin meeting place. And that meant only one thing: Emma wanted to switch places. I tried calling Emma, but she didn't pick up. I texted her and she didn't answer. But we couldn't switch places, could we?

I slowly climbed the ladder and peeked my head out. The first thing I saw was Sydney, smiling and posing in front of a big white screen as Mrs. Burkle took her picture for her headshot. I quietly pulled myself back onto the stage and then bolted for the side door and out into the hallway.

Fortunately, the halls were empty as I raced to the janitor's closet. And there was Emma standing in front of it.

"Ew!" she said. "You smell like the JC and we're not even in it."

"Thanks," I said. "You're helpful."

"Oh, I'll be helpful," she said, and practically shoved me into the JC. "I've got fifteen minutes before mathletes starts. That should be enough time to pose as you and get your picture taken. Your shirt is too wet, but I grabbed your jacket out of your locker on the way. Give me your jeans."

"But we swore not to trade places again," I protested.

"No." Emma looked at me. "No, we didn't."

I remembered how we almost did a pinky swear, but then we'd stopped.

"Besides," Emma said. "We're not *trading* places. I'm just temporarily being you for a few minutes. You're not being me. It's different."

"I'm not? But won't that mean there are two Emmas at the same time?" I asked her. Now that would be weird.

"Not if '*Emma*' stays hidden in the janitor's closet," Emma said. "Hurry up and change and let's get this done!"

So, Emma and I traded outfits. I tossed her my jeans and furry boots. She put on my black jacket. I put on her chocolate-brown sweatpants and sneakers.

"I wish I had worn my spelling bee T-shirt today," Emma said. "You having to wear that would be classic."

No, that would have been just wrong.

"Wait!" I said, looking at her. "Brush your hair for the picture! And put on my barrette!"

Hair was brushed! Barrette was clipped in! Lip gloss was applied!

And . . . Ta-da!

"I'm you!" Emma announced. "I'll go in, get your picture taken, and be back before you know it."

"And I'm supposed to just sit here?" I asked her.

"Excuse me, I'm at risk of missing the first minutes of mathletes to help you," she said.

"You're right," I said. "Hey, Emma? Thanks."

"You're welcome," she said. "And you owe me one."

Emma took a deep breath and walked out the door. I heard one last thing before she disappeared.

"Hi—wait, are you Emma or Payton?" a girl's voice asked.

"Hiiii! I'm Payton!" Emma squealed, totally over the top.

I sat down on a cleaning bucket for the second time today. And sighed.

Emma

Four

MATHLETES . . . ALMOST

Finally. Finally. *Finally.* I was myself again! I checked my watch as I flew through the halls. Eight minutes late. Four hundred eighty precious seconds. But at least I'd made it.

I stopped outside the mathletes room to compose myself. I mussed my hair up a little bit to get back into Emma mode.

Being Payton for her Drama Club pictures had been easy-peasy. I'd given a wide, slightly vacant smile for her headshot. I'd stood in line between Tess and Nick for the group shot.

I'd slipped out, ran to the JC, and quickly switched back with Payton. I'd knocked our secret code knock: *Knock. Knock, tap-tap. Knock!* And then ignored her whining about sitting in the closet for so long. Seriously, I don't know why she was complaining. She could have gotten a lot of homework covered in that free time.

Excellent work, Emma, if I did say so myself.

❀ 36 ❀

However, I'd missed the first few minutes of mathletes. I suddenly felt a moment of nerves as I prepared to walk in late.

Show no fear! I silently repeated my competition mantra and walked confidently into the room. *Show no—*

"What the—!" I was yanked backward. My backpack had gotten caught on the doorknob. My head banged against the door. Ow. I untangled my backpack strap and tried to focus my eyes.

"That's Emma Mills," a girl said loudly. "She has vestibular problems."

I knew that voice. Jazmine James.

"Yeah, Emma, you really should get some special help for that," said a boy.

Of course, it was Hector. Wherever there was Jazmine James, there was Hector.

"I do not have balance problems," I said, shaking off the dizziness. "I told you that last week."

Um, last week—when I accidentally pitched myself over my desk in Science class in front of both Jazmine and Hector. *Grrr . . .*

"Well, Emma," a man's voice boomed. "As long as you do not continue to have punctuality problems and are ready to do some complex mathematics problems, come on in."

I quickly spotted an empty seat in the front row. I loved the front row. I felt my stress melting away. I was a mathlete surrounded by my peers. Oh, yeah. I closed my eyes, wanting to savor.

"What are you doing, making a wish?" Hector's hissing voice barged into my moment. I opened my eyes.

"Emma's wishing she were her twin sister," Jazmine said. "'Cause then she'd have an excuse for all the mistakes she's going to make today."

I turned to my right and glared at Jazmine, then at Hector sitting behind her. My big mistake when I started middle school last week was thinking that Jazmine and I would become friends and partners. Jazmine had won last year's state science fair the same day I won the state spelling bee. So I'd thought she'd appreciate having someone else to talk to at an advanced academic level.

I'd thought wrong. Jazmine was the one who busted Payton and me during our twin switch. Live on schoolwide TV. She had humiliated us—and enjoyed every second of it.

Jazmine James was my evil nemesis. Hector was her henchman.

Well, I reminded myself. This was math. I had been preparing myself for this my whole life and I would take them both down. Mathematically, I meant, not physically.

"Some of you already know me as Mr. Babbitt, your math teacher," the teacher said, interrupting my vengeful thoughts. "But here in mathletes, you are a team. That makes me your coach. In here, you can call me Coach Babbitt."

Fine. All I had to do was focus on Coach Babbitt, formulas, shortcuts, and strategies. No distractions.

"Hey, Emma," someone said from behind me. I froze.

Distraction! Distraction!

Coach Babbitt was busy passing out our fresh new mathlete books, so I turned around.

"Ox?" I asked. Was Ox here?

"Are you okay?" he asked me. Ox reached out and touched my head.

"No lumps," he said. "You look a little dazed, though. I don't think you hit your head enough for a concussion."

Of course I'm dazed! I thought wildly. Ox is here and he is touching me!

"I've seen a few concussions during football," Ox went on. "They can mess you up."

"Football," I said. "Aren't you supposed to be at practice?"

What was Ox doing here?

"Miss Mills," Coach Babbitt said.

I whipped back around and took a workbook. I pretended to look through it studiously, to show the coach I was serious. Actually, I'd already preordered the workbook and done all the problems over summer vacation.

Coach Babbitt moved on to other people.

My mind was swirling. I hadn't seen Ox since yesterday after school when he'd said, *"Emma—I"* and the bell drowned him out and then the whole ox festival fiasco and I was grounded from my phone so he couldn't call me even if he'd wanted to, which he probably didn't because he was apparently saying, "Emma, I . . . am not into you, so, bye."

"Emma, I . . ."—Ox leaned forward and whispered—"told you yesterday that there's no practice today and I hoped I'd see you at mathletes. Remember?"

"Right, sure." I nodded, trying to stay cool. *That* was what he'd said? I was trying to wrap my brain around the fact that Ox might still possibly like me *and* was in mathletes, when some boy in the back started chanting, "Go, Gecko mathletes! Go, Gecko mathletes!"

Everyone started chanting and cheering. I couldn't hear what Ox was saying with all the noise. Did Ox join mathletes to be around me? No, of course not. But was he prepared for this? Poor Ox! He had no idea how complex, how advanced the math was here. Hopefully, he'd just stay quiet and not be humiliated.

"The answer is three," Ox said.

I realized that the whole room had gone quiet. While I was thinking about Ox, everyone else had been thinking about math. What is the maximum number of acute interior angles a convex pentagon can have?

Ox was correct! Ox was mathletes material!

"That is correct," Coach Babbitt said. "Question two, anyone?"

I had to redeem myself, and fast. I had to show the coach and everyone else that I was the mathlete to beat.

"A boat has a speed of six miles per hour in calm water. The boat can travel thirty miles with the current in the same time in which it can travel eighteen miles against the current.

How many hours does it take the boat to travel thirty-six miles against the current?"

Easy! My hand shot up.

"Yes, Emma?" Coach Babbitt said.

"The answer to number two is . . ." I was about to answer my first official mathletes problem!

"Excuse me," someone said from the doorway.

Hey? Who was interrupting my moment? This time I frowned, ready to glare at the perpetrator. I looked over. It was Counselor Case. Oh. I rearranged my face into a smile.

"Greg, I have an emergency situation," said Counselor Case. "I need you to watch the boys."

The boys. There they were. Mason and Jason.

"Sorry about this, honey," Counselor Case said to the coach.

Honey? I watched as she hurried off, leaving the twins in the doorway, punching each other.

"Mason and Jason," Coach Babbitt said. "Go stay by the wall and stay silent."

"But, Dad!" one of the twins said.

Dad?

"We want to sit with Emma!" a twin said.

Sit with Emma?

"I was just about to answer number two—," I said a little desperately.

"Ha-ha! She said 'number two'!" Mason snorted.

I heard another snort. This time from Jazmine James's direction.

"You can't sit with Emma, there aren't any more seats," Coach Babbitt said.

"But Emma's our tutor! Our *math* mentor, who will guide us through the mysteries and joys of math!" Jason said.

Then he and his twin started chanting: "Emma! Emma!"

Please! Would somebody stop this madness?

"Boys, we don't have time for this," Coach Babbitt said.

Whew. He would stop the madness.

"Emma, would you please go sit with the boys to keep the peace," Coach Babbitt said. "Take your workbook and you can participate from there."

So that's how I found myself sitting on the floor against the wall with two eight-year-olds on my first day of mathletes. Because I had to make a good impression on their father—my mathletes coach! And their mother—my guidance counselor! I couldn't even look up to see Jazmine's reaction. Or Hector's. And especially Ox's.

"Now, where were we?" Coach Babbitt asked. "Emma?"

"Number two," I reminded him, then shot a look at Mason and Jason. "I mean, problem two."

Problem two. I had two problems all right. Right next to me. Mason and Jason.

"The answer is eight!" the twin to my left announced.

The whole class burst out laughing.

"Looks like you've got some competition," Jazmine called out.

And everyone laughed. Some more.

Another crushing blow. I leaned back against the wall and tried to block out the embarrassment. I especially didn't look at Ox to see if he was laughing, too. I turned to the minimathletic twin and whispered, "I'll let you use my scientific calculator if you stay quiet."

"Cool!" he said.

"Not fair," the other twin said. "Jason gets a toy. What do I get?"

I sighed and handed him my cell phone, first pressing the mute button and then clicking on my games.

"Math flashcards? Pinball?" Mason said. "You call those games?"

"Problem four," Coach Babbitt said.

Errg. I must have missed them do problem three. I scanned the page to find it.

"It's 142!" Jazmine said.

"Correct!" Coach Babbitt said. "It looks like we're going to have a solid team this year."

And the first mathletes club meeting of the year went on. Every time I raised my hand, a twin would whisper that he needed help or that the screen was frozen. I even had to take them to the bathroom, and it took forever to find the nearest boys' room. When I got back, everyone had packed up. Mathletes was over.

Coach Babbitt was making his way over to me. Behind him, I saw Ox heading out the door. He probably was fleeing from the embarrassment of me. Jazmine and Hector were laughing. Gee, wonder what they were laughing about.

"Emma, I'll take the boys from here," Coach Babbitt said.

Jason started crying. "I want to keep this calculator!" he wailed.

Coach Babbitt groaned.

"You can use mine on the way home, Jason," he said. "And, Mason, hand over the phone."

As Mason reluctantly gave me the phone, I noticed something snaking out of his shirtsleeve.

"Aaaack!" I gasped. "What is that?"

It looked like a tail! A skinny, green tail!

"Nothing," Mason said quickly. "Let's go."

Just as I'd convinced myself it was a loose thread or even a rubber toy, it moved.

"Aaaaack! I mean, um, bye, Coach! Bye, boys!" I grabbed my backpack and coat, and bolted out the door.

"What's her problem?" I heard one twin ask.

"Emma has a problem with her balance," Coach Babbitt replied. "She was probably just a little dizzy."

ACK!!! I screamed inside my head and raced for the dismissal buses. I hoped Payton would save me a seat, so I could hide the whole way home.

Payton

Five

LATE BUS

I bet Emma was sorry I'd saved her a seat. The combination of my stink from the water and the usual stink of the late bus seemed to be overpowering her.

She was leaning as far away from me as she could and still remain on the same bus seat. And she looked kind of sick.

"I'll take a shower as soon as I get home," I told Emma.

"Don't worry about it. I'm almost used to it," Emma said.

"You look like you're going to puke," I told her. "But don't. I don't think we could handle the smell of puke added to this situation."

"I'm not going to puke." Emma sighed. "I'm just feeling nauseated about my mathletes session."

Emma told me about what happened in mathletes. Ouch.

The bus pulled away from the school. I watched the trees and houses whiz by. Emma didn't say anything for a while.

❀ 45 ❀

Neither did I. And then Emma's cell phone rang. She looked surprised. Most of Emma's calls came from me.

"Hello?" Emma said stiffly. "Mm-hmm. Mm-hmm. Certainly. Good-bye." She clicked off.

"Who was that?" I asked her. "Someone trying to sell you something?"

"That was Quinn," Emma said, opening her backpack and pulling out her school planner.

"Quinn?" I asked. "You talked to her like that?"

"Like what?" Emma asked, writing something in her planner.

"I don't know, like a robot," I said. "Hello. This. Is. Emma. Your. Robot. Friend. It didn't sound like you were talking to someone you even knew."

My twin looked at me. Her face was turning pink. She started chewing on her hair. Oops. I had upset her.

"Quinn asked me to go over to her house sometime soon to see her new laptop," Emma said. "I said yes."

"Actually you said 'certainly,'" I said.

"Were my social skills lacking?" Emma asked me quietly.

"Um, kind of," I said. I felt a little bad for Emma. Quinn was her first real friend who seemed to like her for something other than being a brainiac. Or who wasn't trying to get Emma to help with homework. Emma and Quinn had bonded during our twin switch, and afterward Quinn had stopped hanging out with Sydney and Cashmere so much. Quinn seemed nice. I'd hate for Emma to screw it up so fast.

❀ 46 ❀

"Give me your phone," I said to Emma.

"What? Use your own," Emma said.

"No," I said, and grabbed Emma's phone. "This call needs to be from your number."

I ignored Emma's protests as I turned her phone on and pressed "Quinn." I heard Quinn's phone ring.

"Hello?"

"Hey, it's Emma," I said.

Out of the corner of my eye I saw my twin's mouth drop open and her face went all like, *What are you doing?*

I put my finger over my lips.

"Hey, Emma," Quinn said to me.

"Before, when you called?" I said. "I couldn't really talk. Sorry for being so—"

"Abrupt," Emma said, leaning in close to me and finishing my sentence.

I'd been planning to say "lame," but "abrupt" was more Emmaish.

"Abrupt," I repeated. "I can't wait to see your new laptop."

"Cool!" Quinn said. "I have to show you these YouTube videos. They're hilarious."

"Cool!" I said. "Okay, see you."

Quinn said bye and I hung up the phone.

"Payton, you just pretended to be me," Emma said. "Without my permission."

"I was just helping," I said. "You sounded like you were trying to blow her off, so I fixed it. It's no big deal. You just need a little more coaching so you don't destroy your social life."

"Okay, okay," Emma said. "But we're not supposed to pretend to be each other. Especially over something minor."

The bus slowed and pulled over to our stop. My twin sister and I stood up and moved into the aisle.

"Well, I may have to cancel Quinn, anyway," Emma turned to tell me, before stepping down and off the bus. I got off right behind her. "We're grounded."

"Oh, ugh," I said. "I forgot about the grounding. We need to convince Mom and Dad it's time to unground."

And as we walked down our street and up our driveway, we talked fast. By the time we reached our house, we had a plan.

Emma and I were on our best behavior when we got home. We did our homework. I didn't throw my book bag on the floor. That makes my mom crazy. Emma didn't reorganize the mail, which drove my mom crazy.

We even set the table without my mother asking.

"Yum, this chicken is delicious!" I said to my mom.

"You roasted it to perfection," Emma said. "Although if you set the heat a few degrees higher it might help the texture a bit."

I shot her a look.

"But it's delicious!" Emma added.

"Girls, how was school?" my mother asked.

Emma and I looked at each other.

"You didn't switch places again, I hope," my father said, looking at each of us sternly.

"No!" I said.

"Of course not!" Emma said.

We didn't—couldn't—look at each other. We weren't lying to my father. Technically. After school, we'd hung out in our room formulating our plan for "ungrounding." And we decided that we had kept our promise to not switch places.

When Emma took my newspaper photo, I stayed Payton. Therefore, we did not "switch." Emma just substituted. Later, when I called Quinn as "Emma," Emma was still Emma. Again, no switch.

We all ate our chicken and potatoes and peas. Mom worked at home as a writer and researcher and was very serious about her family-eats-dinner-together time. She said it helped a happy family stay together or something.

"School was actually great," I said. "Emma helped me when my locker was stuck!"

"And Payton saved a seat for me on the bus!" Emma added.

"And I think I'm going to do well on my next math test. Thanks to Emma's helping me study after school," I said.

"It was my pleasure," Emma said. "And Payton was very helpful to me after school, too. With . . ."

Come on, Emma. Remember your line.

"With my homework!" Emma finished.

What? There was no way I helped her with her homework! We'd rehearsed this! How can Emma remember long math problems but not her line? My parents looked at us suspiciously.

"Payton helped you with your homework?" my mother asked.

"Uh, well . . . ," Emma said, trying to recover. But it was hopeless.

"So, spit it out. Where are you going with this happy-sister act?" Dad asked.

"Well, there's an educational activity I would like to go to," Emma admitted. "It would give me new technology skills and enhance my social networking opportunities."

"But Emma can't go," I said. "We're grounded."

"Right," Emma said. "So I guess that means I can't go."

Emma sneaked a look at my parents. They continued eating.

"So," I repeated. "I guess that means Emma can't go."

"That wasn't *too* obvious," my dad said. "Emma, just ask."

"Okay. May I please go over to Quinn's house?" Emma asked.

"What is the educational aspect you were talking about?" my mother asked.

"She wants to show me some computer technology," Emma said. "Oh, okay. That's just YouTube videos. She just wants me to come for a social visit."

"But really there's an educational part about it," I said. "Emma needs to learn how to have friends."

"I am glad you're making new friends, Emma," my mom said. "But we take grounding very seriously."

"We do too," I told my mother. "But Emma is already enough of a social freak. She needs to hang out with someone who actually invited her to their house!"

"Isn't that a little harsh?" Emma sputtered.

"Well," my dad said. "I can't remember the last time Emma was invited to someone's house. Wait, does this girl want to copy your homework, Em? You need to be cautious."

"Okay! Forget I asked!" Emma said. "Just because I have valued my academics over social activities in the past—and continue to do so—does not mean the word 'freak' should be involved."

"Sorry," I said. "I didn't mean freak. What's the word I was looking for? Weirdo? Oddball? Loser?" None of them sounded right. . . .

Emma put her head in her hands.

"Enough about poor Emma," my mom said. "I think it's a good idea. Plus, we got an e-mail from Counselor Case today that you both are doing splendidly on your school service jobs."

She looked at my father. He nodded.

"I think we can consider a break from the grounding," my mom said. "But to be really fair, Payton should probably be allowed to go somewhere, too."

Yay! Bonus!

"Friday night is teen night at the skating rink," I suggested.

"I was thinking more along the lines of a study session with a friend at the library," my mother said.

"Or, I could call Tess and we could work on our English paper at the library," I said quickly.

My parents both smiled.

"If you continue to do well, we can discuss ending the punishment period altogether," my mom said.

Yes! Emma and I high-fived across the table.

"I believe you girls are learning your lesson," my father said. "And working as a team."

"We are!" I said. "Identical twins together! Team Emma and Payton! Pemma! Emton! Go, twins!"

Everyone was looking at me. I was getting carried away, wasn't I? I shut up and sat back down.

"Go, Geckos," Emma whispered to me. We cracked up.

Six

AT THE LOCKERS

Last class of the day. Formal academics was done, and now I could use my time more wisely with some choice reading of the classics and more advanced math practice on my own.

I walked down the hall and saw Payton with her head in her locker. I walked up behind her and positioned myself at the perfect angle for my reflection to be in her fuzzy pink locker mirror.

"Ahhhh!" Payton screamed. She whipped her head around. "Emma! You know you freak me out when you do that. It's like I see two me's."

"I know," I said. "I'm working on my freaking-out-other-people skills. I am determined to never be in the situation I found myself in at mathletes yesterday."

"Could you please practice your freaking out on people who deserve it?" Payton asked me. "Now that you actually

❀ 53 ❀

brush your hair, your reflection and mine are too much alike."

"We do look more alike than ever," I mused. "I have to say I was great as you getting your picture taken. Seriously, you should have seen the look on Sydney's face when she saw me—I mean, *you*—walk in perfectly dry and composed."

"Keep it down." Payton looked around. Although the hall was pretty empty, you could never be too careful.

"Then, when the photographer went to take my head-shot and I suggested tilting my head at a twenty-three degree angle instead of a thirty-degree so the light would reflect off my shiny hair—" I continued. "It was brilliant."

"You said *what*?" Payton pulled her head out of her locker. "Yeesh, Emma. Couldn't you just smile?"

"Well," I huffed. "Talk about ungrateful. You'll thank me when your headshot comes back highlighted perfectly."

Payton sighed and pulled out some lip gloss, but then looked at it in disgust.

"Oh, why bother," she groaned. "I'm just going to Drama where I'll be stuck in the basement anyway. I'll probably get some more muddy water dumped on my head."

"Besides, that color is last season," I informed her. "Now that we're heading toward winter, a darker rose is in."

Payton looked at me.

What? Just because I wasn't with Sydney clones didn't mean I shouldn't keep up with the fashion magazines. For sociological-research purposes, that is.

"Drama Club is so depressing," Payton said. "I had to

listen to everyone all happy practicing their lines for the try-outs."

"When are tryouts?" I asked her. "Maybe you'll be done with your school service by then."

"They're today," Payton said sadly. "Today."

"Oh," I said. "Well, perhaps I could pretend to be you once again. One Payton could be cleaning the basement. And the other Payton could be auditioning."

"Yeah, except Mrs. Burkle knows I'm supposed to be in the basement and not auditioning," I said. "Duh."

"I know," I said. "Too bad there wasn't a parallel universe. Then you could be performing your school service and trying out at the same time."

"You're in your EinsteinEmma zone," Payton said. "Which means I have no idea what you're talking about."

"On the other hand," I continued, "I wish there were no Emmas in my parallel universe this afternoon. Then I could be skipping *my* after-school entirely."

I had my first real tutoring session with the boys today after school.

Payton snickered.

"What?" I asked her.

"It's so funny how Jason answered the question for you in mathletes." Payton grinned. "And how Mason said 'number two.' Hah!"

I *so* should not have told her that story.

"Your concept of humor is disturbing," I said. "And also

disturbing is that today I'm tutoring twin horrors who apparently have no shame about humiliating me."

"They're little kids," Payton said. "Not monsters."

"Speaking of monsters, did I tell you about the green tail?" I asked her.

"Um, no," Payton said.

"I swear I saw a green tail come out of one of their shirt-sleeves." I shuddered. I had a nightmare last night about twin giant green monsters attacking me with their tails.

"Now *you* sound disturbed. I think you need to get more sleep," Payton said.

Payton pulled off her hoodie, so she just had a plain white long-sleeved T-shirt on. The hoodie was one of her Summer Slave clothes.

"No sense in ruining my cute hoodie when I'm cleaning," Payton explained.

"Hah, you're changing out of your Summer Slave clothes so you can be a Stage Slave!" I said.

"Now *your* concept of humor is disturbing," Payton said.

"Stage Slave," I teased her.

"Number two," she shot back.

"Hi, Payton! Hi, Emma!" The voice behind us made us both jump.

Oh. Tess.

"Hi, Tess," I said tensely.

I didn't completely trust Tess. I'd met Tess first as one of Jazmine James's sidekicks. Tess had told me she'd known

Jazmine and Hector since they were the three kindergartners in their school's gifted-and-talented program.

"So, are you nervous or excited?" Tess asked Payton.

"For what?" I asked her.

"For play tryouts!" Tess said. "Didn't Payton tell you we have tryouts today?"

Yes, however, apparently Payton hadn't told Tess that she couldn't try out.

"I'm both nervous and excited," Tess said. "I had a nightmare last night that I was up onstage and I threw up in front of everyone. What if that really happens?"

"Then Payton will clean up the vomit," I said.

"Emma!" Payton said.

"Payton, just tell her," I said. "She's going to find out anyway."

"It's so humiliating," Payton said. She hid her face in her locker.

"Payton can't try out for the play because her school service is cleaning the filthy drama supply room," I explained. "That's where she disappeared to yesterday during class."

"You have to clean?" Tess asked Payton. "You can't try out?"

"No," Payton said. "I was going to tell you, of course, but I felt so stupid."

"I thought you were just getting ready for the headshots when you were gone," Tess said. "When you came back for your picture your hair looked so nice and shiny. . . ."

"Thank you," I said under my breath.

Payton shot me a dirty look. Well, hey. That *was* my hair that was clean and shiny. I'd read about this new conditioner in one of Payton's fashion magazines. I, of course, was skeptical about ads, especially in teen magazines. However, the ingredient list caught my eye. And it truly did make my hair extra shiny. I'd have to recommend it to Payton.

"So, anyway, Payton can't try out," I said to Tess. "But, Tess, that's good news for you. Less competition."

"I don't care about that," Tess said sadly. "I want Payton to be in the play with me!"

"Hmm," I wondered out loud. "You really aren't a Jazmine James clone, are you? Jazmine would take out the competition in an instant. Jazmine would be thrilled. Jazmine would be—"

"—coming down the hall," Payton said. "Shush."

Jazmine, followed by Hector, *was* coming our way. I did my calming breathing trick as Jazmine straightened up tall. She was seriously intimidating in her crisp white shirt and tall black boots.

"I love those boots," Payton blurted out.

"Thanks, Payton," I muttered. "So helpful."

"I heard you were here," Jazmine said to Tess, ignoring both Payton and me. "I came to see if you'd changed your mind and come to your senses about choosing Drama over mathletes. You're not really going to audition and commit your time to frivolity, are you?"

"Yes," Tess said quietly.

"I'm disappointed," Jazmine said. "Mathletes needs you. Our team is looking somewhat weak."

"Well, Emma's on it," Payton said loyally. "She's the reigning champion of our old school."

"Emma *was* what I was referring to as 'weak,'" Jazmine said.

"Maybe Emma will improve since she's being tutored by those little boy twins," Hector said, and he and Jazmine cracked up.

"You guys . . . ," Tess said.

Interesting. She was actually going to stick up for me? Well. No need for her to face the wrath of Jazmine. This was my battle and I intended to prevail. I stepped in front of Tess and looked at Jazmine, using my best stare-down technique—the one normally reserved for sudden death rounds of academic competitions.

"Insults are the sincerest form of jealousy," I said. "So Tess and I thank you both for your correct perception of the inevitable."

Jazmine took a step back.

"And Jazmine?" I added. "Your boots would look better with a slightly shorter skirt. That length makes your body appear unbalanced."

Jazmine's eyes flickered down to her skirt. Ha! Score!

"Come on, Hector," Jazmine said. She turned and swished away, Hector on her heels.

"I didn't understand the first part, but the part about the boots was awesome," Payton said to me. "She was speechless!"

"Yeah, actually the first part didn't make a whole lot of sense," I admitted, feeling a little shaky still.

"But effective, nonetheless!" Tess said, smiling at me.

I turned to Tess and smiled back. "Thanks for trying to stick up for me, Tess," I said. "But I needed to do that on my own. I can't show weakness. Good luck with your tryouts. And, well, Payton, good luck with your . . . cleaning."

"And, Emma, good luck with the tutor-twins," Payton said, and waved.

Okay. I felt a little bit better now. If I could handle Jazmine James, I just might be able to handle those boys.

Seven

DRAMA/SCHOOL SERVICE

"Payton, I feel terrible," Tess said. "We need to talk to Mrs. Burkle and get you an audition."

"Thanks, but nope," I said. "I have to do my school service hours. Trust me, my alternative is detention, and I can't risk that."

"I think it's too harsh," Tess said. "First you're off VOGS for two weeks and now this? I was really looking forward to being in the play with you."

"Well," I said. "I'll still be nearby, cheering you on."

Okay, I might be underneath everyone, cheering them on. I felt a little more cheerful, though. Tess was turning into a new friend. I really would cheer her on. I just wished she could return the favor.

We headed into the auditorium. Tess went to a seat and gave me a sad face as I went up the steps and behind the curtain. I found the trapdoor in the floor and climbed down the ladder.

I texted Tess:

Break a leg!

Okay, it was time to get to work. I looked around the room. It was still a total disaster. I decided I would organize the huge pieces of wood that were used on the sets. One was an old giant fake tree that had peeling paint. One was a platform on wheels, so I rolled it off to the side. And I noticed another ladder along the wall leading up to another trapdoor.

I climbed up and pushed it open. A beam of light came through.

"There's no place like home!" I heard someone say dramatically.

Oh my gosh! I'd pushed the door open onto the stage! I'd just heard someone auditioning. I quickly closed the door. Then I pushed it open a little bit, just so I could hear. I noticed a latch and fastened it on. The door stayed open a crack and I could hear the wanna-be Dorothy.

"Oh, Auntie Em! There's no place like home!"

I heard applause. I paused to think about what part I would have tried out for. Definitely not Dorothy. I was not that talented. It would be fun to play someone evil, like the Wicked Witch.

"Next up, Sydney," Mrs. Burkle announced.

Ha! I was just thinking of the Wicked Witch and—I laughed, and then covered my mouth. I didn't want to get busted.

"Thank you, Mrs. Burkle. I'd like to audition for the role of Glinda, the Good Witch," Sydney said.

I debated shutting the trapdoor and saving myself the misery of hearing it.

"Are you a good witch or a bad witch?" Sydney's voice rang out.

Sydney had the sweetness down. It was amazing that someone so mean could sound so sweet.

"Wonderful!" Mrs. Burkle said.

And amazing how that same person could make adults think they were so sweet. Sydney = Glinda, definitely not!

I climbed back down the ladder and started moving things around. I cleaned and organized as I listened to the people trying out for different parts. I heard potential Scarecrows, Cowardly Lions, and Tin Men.

And then I heard Mrs. Burkle call Tess's name. I climbed quickly back up the ladder and held my breath.

"I'd like to read for Auntie Em," Tess said, her voice wavering.

Auntie Em? I tried to picture Tess as Dorothy's aunt. Then she started to read Auntie Em's lines, and . . .

Wow. Tess was good. Really good. I listened to her for a while and smiled. Tess had a good shot at a part, I thought.

"Next up, Reilly Hamilton," Mrs. Burkle said.

I heard a boy get up and introduce himself.

"Tess, I need someone to read against Reilly," Mrs. Burkle said. "Can you just pop up here and please read Dorothy's lines while Reilly reads for The Scarecrow?"

"Payton!" a voice called down from the other side of the room. It was Zahra!

I closed the trapdoor and scrambled down the ladder. And I missed a rung, and fell flat on my butt.

Ow.

"Oh, sorry! I didn't see you," Zahra said. "Mrs. Burkle said you can come up now. They're almost finished."

"Thanks," I said. I got up off the floor and walked gingerly over to the ladder. Ow. I was pretty sure I was going to be black and blue. I climbed slowly up the ladder, and came out onstage just as most everyone had packed up their stuff and started to leave. People were high-fiving and hugging each other. Everyone was excited and bonding and having so much fun.

Ow.

Then I saw Tess coming toward me. I forced a grin. Well, it wasn't too hard. I was genuinely happy for her. I was just bummed I didn't get my own chance.

"Congratulations!" I slid off the stage and ran up to her. "You were awesome!"

"You heard me?" Tess asked.

"Yes, and you were great!" I said. "Mrs. Burkle even had you read lines with some boy. That's a good sign, right?"

"Do you think?" Tess asked, unsure. "I think it was because I was the last person, that's all."

"Tess, you were really good," said a voice from behind me. I recognized the voice of the boy who read for the Lion. I turned around and saw a supercute boy with dark blond hair and blue eyes standing there.

"So were you," Tess squeaked. "Reilly."

"Good luck!" he said, smiling at both of us.

We watched for a second as he went over and joined his friend.

"Okay, he is cute," I whispered. "Seriously cute."

"I know, I was shaking so hard when I was reading with him," Tess said. "He looks like a movie star."

Oh, why can't I be in this play? Great roles. Cute boys. Costumes. Hugging and high-fiving and audience applause! And I was missing out.

"Hey, wait a minute," the boy who was over with Reilly called out, and came over to us.

"*Squeee!*" I squeal-whispered to Tess.

"My friend and I were talking about you," he said—and stopped in front of me. Me!

I looked at Tess. She was like, *Oh my gosh!!!*

"Reilly is shy," the boy said to me. "I told Reilly I'd ask you a question."

What! What was the question? Was he . . . going to see if I'd go out with Reilly? Ask me to practice lines with Reilly? Ask me to be his leading lady for the rest of our lives?

❀ 65 ❀

"Is it true that you and your twin sister were Siamese twins and stuck together by your ears?" he asked.

"What!" I said. I *so* could not believe he just asked that. I felt myself turning bright red.

"Oh my gosh, that is not true," Tess said. "It's not true, right?"

"Duh! Of course it's not true," I said.

Reilly came up to us.

"Hey," he said.

Ah! Cuteness!

"I'm not a Siamese twin," I blurted out.

"Uh . . ." He gave me a weird look. "Okay."

Awkward silence. Then the other boy started laughing really hard.

"You didn't tell him to ask me if I was once attached to my sister at the ears?" I asked Reilly.

"Uh, no," he said. He turned to the other boy. "Charlie, you're a dork."

The Charlie guy was laughing so hard he fell into a seat.

"Ignore my friend," Reilly said to me.

Gladly.

Emma

Eight

LIBRARY AFTER SCHOOL

"Focus," I said, "on the fun of solving math problems."

Four identical eyes stared at me. Mason and Jason were sitting across the small rectangular library table from me.

I gave my intimidation stare back, but it didn't work. I lowered my eyes down to the papers I'd laid out on the table.

"So, um, Jason," I said. "Here's a set of warm-up problems from mathletes. You can work on these while I work with Mason."

One of the twins reached out and took the paper. (Okay, so that one is apparently Jason.)

Jason started on the math sheet without complaint. Whew. One down. One twin to go.

"Mason, we're going to learn the multiplication tables today!" I said, feigning enthusiasm.

"What fun!" Mason said, mimicking my cheeriness.

"Actually, it is kind of fun to fill out the table," I said. Not fake cheery, just being myself. "There are lots of cool patterns. Let's start with the twos. Just skip count."

As both boys wrote on their pages, I surveyed the library. I was looking around for the library media specialists, hoping they'd notice what a good role model I was.

I imagined a conversation with Counselor Case:

CC: I heard wonderful things about your tutoring
     session, Emma. The library media specialists
     told me what a great role model you are.
Me (modestly): Oh, it was nothing.
CC: Thanks to you, both my boys scored in the highest
     percentile for math *and* they both say when they
     grow up they want to be just like you.

Smiling, I leaned over and looked at Mason's multiplication table. Wha-huh? Instead of 2, 4, 6, 8, 10, and so on, I saw 4, 16, 36, 64, 100 . . . ! And in the 3's row? Not 3, 6, 9, but 27, 216, 729, and 1,728!

"Mason!" I said. "What are you doing?"

"I'm squaring the twos and cubing the threes," he said, still writing. "Next, I'll do the fours to the fourth power. So I need to borrow your calculator."

Oh. Kay. Tutor must stay in control.

"Erm, Jason?" I said. "May I see your worksheet?"

The other twin handed me the mathletes warm-up sheet.

There were no answers on it at all. Just doodles of vehicles.

"Sssooo," I said slowly. "The volume of a sphere with a radius of seven is a . . . car?"

"Hello? Not just a car. A Lamborghini," the doodle twin said.

I took a deep breath.

"Boys," I said. "Do you do this often?"

"Do what?" they both asked me.

"Don't play innocent with me," I growled. "You know what I mean. Switch places."

Mason/Jason and Jason/Mason both started giggling. They gave each other high-fives.

"Guys, you know your mom really wants you to behave," I said. "What made you think this was a good idea?"

"You did it," said one twin to me.

"Yeah, you and your sister fooled the whole school," the other twin said. "We heard my mom and the other counselor freaking out about it. We decided to practice on you and then take it to a wider audience."

"No, no, no." I put my head in my hands. "I'm supposed to be a role model for *math,* not for twin chaos. Look, switching places was a big—no, HUGE—mistake. And in the end you're only hurting yourselves."

And, wasting my time.

"Well, Mason, I believe we've been admonished," the twin formerly known as Mason said.

"Well, Jason, I believe you're still a doofus," said Mason.

Suddenly, both boys jumped out of their seats and started beating on each other.

"Stop!" I hissed. "This is the library!"

And just as quickly, the boys stopped and hopped back in their seats.

"Fake fight." Jason smiled at me.

"Psych." Mason smiled at me. "Man, I can't believe she busted us that easy."

"Easily. And this means extra homework for both of you." I smiled back. Ha! Three could play at this twins game.

Fortunately, the boys took me seriously after that. I handed them fresh worksheets and ordered them to get back to work. I felt frazzled and a little sweaty. I unclipped a binder clip from my papers and used it to clamp my hair off my neck. Payton would be unhappy with my fashion-meets-function choice, but hey.

And then . . . there he was. Ox. Ox was in the library. Ox was looking around the library. Ox was looking at me! And grinning!

I casually leaned over to check Mason's paper so Ox could see what a hard-working tutor I was.

"Nice job, Mason," I said. "Except your six is written backward."

I pointed to the error. And then it happened. Something popped out of Mason's long sleeve and jumped onto my hand. It was the owner of the green tail. And its beady little eyes were staring at me.

"Eep!" I squeaked. I shook my hand. "Get it off me!"

Whatever "it" was flew off my hand.

"Ohmigosh," I breathed. "What was that? Where'd it go?"

"In your hair," Jason said. "Don't move."

In. My . . .

"AUUUUHHHH!" I whispered, not wanting to attract a library media specialist's attention.

"It's in my hair," I wailed as softly as I could, feeling around my head. Hair. Hair. Get it out.

"It's a gecko," Mason said softly.

I looked at him. A gecko? Our school mascot? It was one thing to be surrounded by cartoon geckos on posters cheering on the football team. Cartoon geckos are harmless and two-dimensional. But real living, breathing, crawly, slithery reptiles freaked me out.

Yes, I have herpetophobia: fear of reptiles.

"You have a gecko?" I asked, taking a deep breath and attempting not to hyperventilate.

"It's the gecko from the science lab!" Mason said cheerfully.

"It's a bribe," Jason added. "My mom said we can take him every day you tutor us so we'll behave."

"We're not allowed to have pets at home, so it's like he's my pet," Mason said.

"*Our* pet." Jason frowned.

"Mostly mine," Mason said. "He likes me best."

"I don't care who he likes best as long as it's not me," I said through gritted teeth. "Get it out of my hair."

Mason put his hands in my hair and tugged. And tugged.

"Ouch, I meant get the gecko out, not my hair," I said.

"He won't come out," Mason said.

"He's clinging to the clip in your hair with his suction toes. He's gripping on tight. And, his tail is tangled in your hair," Jason observed.

Could this be any worse? Yes, yes it could.

"Geckos have toe pads that adhere to most surfaces," Ox said.

Ox. OX! Ox had come up to our table. I was caught by the boy of my dreams with a gecko stuck on my head. Definitely worse.

"All surfaces except Teflon," Jason corrected him.

"Could we please stop with the reptile trivia? It's trapped in my hair!" I said. I started feeling slightly panicky and dizzy. My breath started going in and out in shorter gasps. Perfect. I was going to hyperventilate, pass out, and end up lying comatose on the floor with a gecko in my hair.

Ox slowly cupped his hands around my head and said, *"Come on, little gecko."*

Ox pulled his hands away, still closed.

"Got him," he said. After he handed the creature back to Mason, he leaned toward me.

"Emma, are you okay?" he asked.

"Go, gecko," I said weakly. And this time, I meant it literally.

A few hours later, I was home in our bedroom sitting on my bed. I had my science book out, but I couldn't concentrate

on it. I looked over at Payton, who was laughing hysterically.

"Okay, tell me again," she said. "You were sitting there
with a real live gecko on your head and Ox said what?"

"Something about the sticky pads of a gecko's feet," I said
grumpily. "Remember, Ox knows a lot about animals. That's
how he got his nickname."

She could stop laughing now.

"Okay, okay." I threw my pillow at her. It missed. "May
we change the subject? What about *your* school service? Any
more drama at Drama?"

Payton grew quiet.

"Just the usual," she said. "I did the dirty work. Everyone
else had fun. Oh, Tess was amazing in her audition. She got to
read lines with this supercute boy."

"Who?" I asked. Ox had been really nice to me after rescuing me from the gecko attack. It would be nice if Payton also
had a boy, well, not a boyfriend, exactly. But a boy who was
more than just a regular friend like Ox and me.

"His name is Reilly," Payton said. "He's an eighth grader."

"Well, at least you can look at him onstage instead of
Sydney," I said.

"Ugggh, Sydney." My sister made a gagging noise. "Now
I'm going to have nightmares."

"Girls!" My mom poked her head into the room. "Time
for bed."

"Okay, Mom," I said. I put my science book on the bedside

table. No begging to stay up later to study. I yawned. It had been a long day.

"Pay—" I started to say good night, when, *whop!* Something soft hit my face.

"You'll need your pillow," my sister said. "Good night, Emma."

"No! No geckos!" someone was yelling.

"Emma!" I heard Payton say.

"Twin geckos are attacking me!" I wailed. "Red-headed geckos that want me to tutor them in math!"

"Oh, yeesh. Wake up, Emma. Wake. Up."

"I'll wake up when you get these twin geckos off me!" I wailed.

"Emma," Payton said. "Open your eyes."

I opened my eyes. I was in my bedroom. Apparently, no twin geckos were attacking me. I swatted at my head to be sure.

"You were dreaming," Payton said. "Loudly."

"Oh." I shuddered. "I was surrounded by these geckos who had red hair and freckles and were trying to suction my brains out with their suction feet."

"Okay, ew," Payton said. "But still not a good enough excuse to wake me up in the middle of the night."

"I'm freaked out," I whimpered. "Payton, it seemed so real. This is too much for me."

"Just ask the boys not to bring the gecko," Payton said.

"I can't," I said. "As a bribe their mom told them they could bring it every time I tutor them. Every time! I cannot handle this."

Payton turned on her bedside lamp and looked at me.

"You're right," she said. "You can't handle this. You should tell Counselor Case."

"Tell Counselor Case?" I said. "Absolutely not! If she thinks I can't handle her sons, she'll think I can't handle pressure! She holds my life—and the ability to place me in advanced high school classes, thereby determining my success in getting into a highly competitive college—in her hands! And she'll tell her husband, Coach Babbitt, and he'll pull me from mathletes and—"

"Emma! Deep breath!" Payton interrupted. "Okay, how about if I help you. I'll take one of the twins—and the gecko—for you next time. And I'll try to talk the twin into not bringing the gecko anymore. Then they'll blame it on me and not you."

"Hmm," I said. That was a good idea. And I had another good idea. "You can take Mason."

"Isn't Mason the one who needs the tutoring?" Payton asked. "The reason you're doing this?"

"You're right." I sighed. "I'll take Mason."

He was obviously the more difficult twin, but it was still better than any twin + gecko, for sure.

"I must be delirious from lack of sleep, but I'll do that for you if you stop waking me up with those nightmares," Payton said. "And you need sleep, too. Your beauty sleep."

"MY beauty sleep? What about you?" I asked.

"I just need sleep," Payton shot back. "The beauty part is already taken care of."

"Har, har," I said. "But, hello, we're identical, so that doesn't make sense."

I waited for a comeback but just heard light snoring sounds. Payton was already asleep. I decided to send Counselor Case an e-mail first thing in the morning. I'd suggest that a session focusing on Mason would be good for his math self-esteem. I'd also say that Payton was . . . envious . . . of my time with the boys and would like to take Jason. It would be perfect! Checking my hair one last time for geckos, I pulled the covers over my head and went back to sleep.

Payton

Nine

LOCKERS AFTER LAST PERIOD

"Do I have dark circles under my eyes?" Emma asked me as we opened our lockers after last period.

"I have concealer if you need it," I said. Then I stopped to look at her. "Since when do you care if you have circles under your eyes?"

"Well, as you *know,* I didn't get much sleep last night," Emma said.

"I know," I told her. "But you look fine."

"Phew," Emma said. "I didn't want Jazmine James to think I was losing sleep worrying about mathletes. I want to look fresh and on my game. I'm so glad I don't have to tutor the boys today."

"I am too," I said. "Since I made that half-asleep promise to take Jason for you."

Sigh. I did regret my offer to take one of the twins off her hands. But at least it wasn't today.

❀ 77 ❀

"Counselor Case told me it was fine. She told the boys that Jason will go with you next time and Mason will stay with me."

"Fine, I'm just glad it's not today," I said. "I'll be under the stage cleaning. *And* I'll hear everyone getting their parts."

The roles were being announced for *The Wizard of Oz*. I, of course, would be happy for everyone. Just sad for me. The first big play and I didn't even get to try out.

I sighed as I shoved my "school clothes" into my locker. Today I was going to clean behind the shelves—a particularly dirty job. So, into my locker went my Summer Slave light blue tank and my purchased-by-Emma-when-she-was-pretending-to-be-me-at-the-mall gray cardigan. I was now wearing an oversized green T-shirt from my summer camp over my jeans. I pulled my hair up into a ponytail.

"No comment on my clothes," I said to Emma. "Nobody's going to see me under the stage."

"*I'm* not the twin who comments on fashion choices," Emma said.

"I have a serious mess to clean up today," I continued grumbling. "And *I'm* exhausted. You weren't the only one who didn't get sleep last night with you having nightmares and shouting 'Geckos!'"

"Geckos! Geckos!" someone yelled.

Emma and I both looked at each other.

"That was weird," Emma said.

"Oh, no," I said. "There's *my* gecko nightmare."

Sydney was walking our way, followed by Cashmere. Sydney was in her green-and-yellow cheerleading outfit.

"Go, Geckos!" she shouted, and kicked a cheer jump.

I quickly got my backpack, hoping I could escape before Sydney passed us.

"Ew, it's the twins," I heard. Suddenly a green pom-pom landed at my feet.

Too late.

"Ooopsie!" Sydney said. "Dropped my pom."

"Ignore," Emma said under her breath.

I couldn't help it. I gave the pom-pom a flying kick.

"Payton, you better hurry up or you're going to be late for Drama," Sydney said, scooping up her pom-pom. "We're finding out the cast today! Oh, wait, you couldn't try out."

Cashmere laughed. Erg.

"Hey, Cashmere," Emma suddenly called out. "How come you didn't try out for Drama? Sydney tell you not to because she's afraid of competition?"

I had to give Emma credit. She was not backing down from Sydney. Unlike me, who was practically hiding in my locker.

"No," Cashmere said. "Sydney told me not to because— wait, why couldn't I try out, Syd?"

"Oh, puh-lease, like you'd be competition," Sydney said. "I mean, because you're so busy with your other . . . activities."

"Oh, what are you involved in, Cashmere?" Emma asked.

"Well, we go to the mall Wednesdays and Fridays and . . .

um . . . ," Cashmere said, looking suspiciously at Sydney.

"Whatever," Sydney said. "What *are* you wearing, Payton? I thought you were supposed to be the fashionable twin. Oh, that's right. You have to clean the basement."

"Oh, look, I have a text!" Emma said, cutting her off.

"It's probably Ox," I said.

Sydney's eyes narrowed. *Zing!*

"Come on, Cash," Sydney said. "Let's go find out what part I have in the play."

They trotted off down the hall. *Ergh.*

"So who was the text really from?" I asked Emma.

"There was no text, genius. I was saving you. And then you had to go say that about Ox? I can't believe you said it might be Ox," Emma said, and then groaned. "So embarrassing. And what if Sydney says something to him?"

I knew Emma felt like she was on shaky ground with Ox.

"Sorry," I said. "I choked. But it got rid of Sydney, didn't it? It was the only thing I could think of to bother her."

The bell rang.

"Okay, can't be late for mathletes!" Emma said. "See you on the late bus!"

I wished I could be late for Drama. In fact, I wished I didn't have to go at all. I went down the hall and stairs toward the auditorium.

I walked into the auditorium and went straight for the door leading under the stage before anyone could see me. I looked around. I decided to dust the shelves in the back first.

Dusting. Dusting.

Coughing. Coughing.

Wiping dirt off face. Realizing that wiping face with dusty hand only gets things dirtier.

Wipe dirty hands on shirt.

Whew. Once again, I thought of Cinderella in the ashes, dressed in rags.

"Payton," someone called. It was Mrs. Burkle, the Drama teacher, sticking her face through the ceiling hole. "I forgot to tell you. The janitor is fumigating the storage room below, so you won't have to clean today."

"Oh!" I said, and then coughed up some dust. "So should I just go home or what?"

"You may join the rest of the Drama group for the day," Mrs. Burkle said.

Yay! I'd get to be a part of things! But, boo! I was covered in dirt and dressed in rags. I couldn't be seen like this.

"I can go to the library or something instead," I suggested.

"No need. It will be short, anyway," she went on. "We can't stay in the auditorium once the fumigation begins. I'll just announce the cast list and everyone can leave. Come join us."

Swell.

I was going to ask if I could go change and wash up first, but her face disappeared. So I climbed back upstairs and went out to the stage. I hoped nobody noticed me. I spotted Tess and quickly went over to the row she was sitting in.

"I'm so glad you're here," Tess said.

"At least I can cheer you on," I told her, scrunching down in my seat so nobody would see how gross I was.

"I'd be a lot more excited if you could have tried out, too," Tess said.

"Yeah, you were really good at VOGS," Nick said, turning around from the seat in front of me. "You were really comfortable talking to people."

"Aw, thanks," I said, sitting up straight. "Are you dying to know what part you got?"

"Actually, I'm tech manager," he said. "I didn't try out for a part. I just want to do the lighting, special effects, all that stuff."

"Oh, good luck with it," I told him.

"No luck needed." He smiled. "I was the only one who wanted the job."

I remembered how good he was at the VOGScast. He'd be great at it. He turned back, facing ahead.

I smiled and smoothed my hair back. And my hair got stuck in a tangle, reminding me I was all dirty and gross and was supposed to be hiding from people. I scrunched back down in my seat.

Tess was looking around and nervously biting her nails.

"You're nervous?" I asked her.

"More nervous than the mathletes competition," she said. "More nervous than the spelling bee. More nervous than the science fair. Isn't that silly? Jazmine would laugh if she could see me now."

"No, it just means you must really want a part," I said.

"What? I can't really hear you down there," Tess said, and leaned over. "Why are you all crunched down?"

"Hello?" I pointed to myself. "I'm dirty and gross?"

"Oh, it's not like anyone would notice," Tess said. Her cell rang and she answered it.

Suddenly, a pom-pom was being waved in my face.

"Ew! What are you wearing, Payton?" Sydney asked, learning across the aisle. "Yeesh. Even your twin sister dresses better than that! And is that dirt on your face?"

Figures Sydney would notice. I turned to see Tess's reaction, but she was turned the other way, talking on her phone.

"Are you even allowed to be here, Payton? Aren't you supposed to be in the dungeon?" Sydney slid into the seat in the front row right in front of us.

"Payton doesn't have to today!" Tess said, now off her phone call and turning back around.

"Oh, so your torture is to wait and hear everyone's name being called but yours." Sydney sighed dramatically to me. "So harsh."

"It is," Tess agreed.

Tess was too nice to see that Sydney was rubbing it in on purpose. Sydney was too good at faking being nice.

"Excuse me, who are you?" Sydney asked Tess.

"I'm Tess," Tess said, smiling.

"Tess is the one who did that great audition as Auntie Em," I said. "With that boy Reilly. Remember?"

"Vaguely." Sydney shrugged. Then she perked up. "Ooh! Look who's here! Our leading man!"

I looked over to see Reilly walking down the aisle. Tess and I both went, *sigh*. He was seriously cute.

"He's so hot." Sydney sighed.

Yup.

Sydney took a pom-pom and waved it over her head to catch Reilly's attention.

"Ooh!" she said. "He's coming over!"

Reilly sat down a few seats from Sydney next to some other boys.

"Reilly! Reilly! Are you dying to know what part you'll get?" Sydney called over to him.

"Sure. Dying," he said. Then he wrapped his hands around his neck and acted out a dramatic death scene, collapsing on his chair. His friend next to him cracked up.

"You're such a good actor!" Sydney squealed. "I wish I could have tried out for a lead. But I can't, because I'm also a *cheerleader*."

Sydney shook her pom-pom.

"Mrs. Burkle said she'd let me try out for a smaller role, though." She smiled at him.

"Cool." He turned back to talk to his friend.

Sydney looked annoyed about losing his attention.

"At least *I* got to try out, though, right, Payton?" she said, aiming her annoyedness right at me.

"You may not realize this, but Payton is already sad about

that," Tess said to Sydney. "You may not want to rub it in."

Oh, Sydney realized it all right.

"Oh, look!" I interrupted loudly. "Mrs. Burkle is onstage with the cast list!"

Everyone turned their attention to the teacher onstage. She was carrying a clipboard. Suddenly the room—including Sydney—fell quiet.

"I'm happy to share the cast list with you," Mrs. Burkle said. "This was a tough decision and remember that all of you are fabulous! Simply superb!"

I reached over and squeezed Tess's hand as Mrs. Burkle started announcing the cast. She read off Munchkins and Flying Monkeys.

"Glinda, the Good Witch will be played by Sydney Fish," she said.

"*Eeee!*" Sydney squealed and clapped. "I'm so thrilled and honored!"

Mrs. Burkle read out a bunch of names, and other people clapped and screamed.

"And The Scarecrow will be Reilly," she said.

Reilly stood up and bowed as we applauded.

"And Dorothy will be . . . Tess Hartwick," she announced.

"Oh my gosh!" Tess said. "Oh!"

"Congratulations!" I said, along with a bunch of other kids. Tess got the lead!

"You're going to be a great Dorothy," I told her.

"If you didn't get a part and would like to join Nick on

tech crew, let me know," Mrs. Burkle said. "Cast, please pick up your scripts on the way out so you can memorize your lines."

Then she told us we had to leave the auditorium because the janitor was spraying it. She said we could go to the library or cafeteria until the late buses.

"We got killed with math homework, didn't we, Nick?" Tess asked. "I should probably go to the library."

"Duh, we should go to the cafeteria! You have to be quiet in the library," Sydney said.

Sydney was talking to us. Why was Sydney talking to us? Or sitting with us? Then I realized Sydney didn't have any friends at Drama.

"Let's hit the library," Reilly was saying to his friend as they got up to leave.

"Or, the library's a good idea," Sydney said, also hearing Reilly. "Let's go."

We all walked in a big clump to the library. People were congratulating each other or cheering up people who didn't get a part. Some people came to talk to Nick about working on the tech crew. People congratulated Sydney and Tess. I walked quietly with them.

Tess, Nick, and I went over to a library table between the book stacks. Sure enough, Sydney came over to sit with us. She pulled up a chair between Nick and Tess.

"We should start memorizing our lines," Sydney said, pulling out the script.

"Wow, Tess, you have a ton of lines," I said, looking at her. "But with your brain you'll totally be able to memorize fast."

Tess blushed.

"Tess is in all honors classes with my sister," I said to Sydney. "She's supersmart."

"Oh, you're a brainiac?" Sydney asked. "You don't look like one. Okay, so let's practice our lines. Here's the part where Glinda floats down in the bubble to see Dorothy. Nick, you'll make me a good bubble for my grand entrance, right?"

"I'm not sure I'm good enough to make a bubble," Nick said. "Especially one that floats."

"Oh, you'll figure it out." Sydney dismissed him, like *pfft!* "Okay, here's our scene. Payton, you can play the weird little Munchkins."

Um, what?

"'Are you a good witch or a bad witch?'" Sydney said dramatically.

"Hold on," Tess said, flipping her script open. "Okay, here's my line. 'Who me? Why, I'm not a witch at all. I'm Dorothy Gale from Kansas.'"

She held her script open for me.

"'Ooooh,'" I said, reading my Munchkin lines. "'Eeeeh!'"

"Hey, are you guys practicing?" a deep voice asked us. "Can I join you?"

We all looked up and saw Reilly standing over us. He ran his hand through his brown hair and smiled with his perfectly white teeth.

Oooooh. Eeeh! Because he sat down in the chair next to me. I could almost touch his arm with my elbow. *Ooooh! Eeeeh!*

"She"—Sydney pointed to me—"was just reading the Munchkin lines. Payton, too bad you have to be the janitor. You'd be a great little Munchkin."

I turned red.

"There's a janitor in *The Wizard of Oz*?" Reilly looked confused.

"Hey!" Nick saved me. "Let's go to the place in the script where Reilly is. Scarecrow, right?"

"Yeah," Reilly said. He flopped over like a scarecrow, and grinned.

I sneaked a look sideways at him. He was so cute. And he was sitting next to me! *Squee!*

"Oh, Glinda and The Scarecrow aren't in too many scenes together." Sydney pouted.

Too bad, so sad.

"Reilly. Maybe we can practice our lines together," Sydney said.

"That makes no sense, since, as you said, you guys are hardly in any scenes together," Nick pointed out. "Tess and Reilly should practice together."

"Oh, Tess won't need practice, since she's such a genius, like you said, Payton," Sydney shot back. "I can read lines for someone else, too."

The Tin Man? Since he's missing a heart?

"What?" Sydney looked at me.

Oh, crud. I said that out loud.

"She said The Tin Man, who is missing a heart," Nick said. "Right, Payton?"

"Right," I said weakly.

"So why didn't you try out for a part?" Reilly asked me.

Oh! Oh! Reilly was gazing at me with his blue eyes. His long eyelashes. And, ugh, asking me a question I *so* did not want to answer.

"I bet you would have been really good, Payton," Reilly continued. "Since you were so good on the school news."

I almost passed out right then and there. He knew who I was! He knew who I was!

"Eep," I squeaked. "I mean, thanks."

"Did you see her on VOGS fighting with her twin?" Sydney asked innocently.

I glared at her.

"Yeah, that's so cool you're identical twins," Reilly said.

I changed my glare to a triumphant smile. Sydney frowned.

"I could tell you guys apart anytime," he said to me. "Even today, when you're both wearing ponytails and old T-shirts. Well, she's got on a mathletes shirt and you've got on a camp shirt, but you're pretty much dressed the same."

What? He knew all that? I started to get a stupid grin on my face. He knew what we both were wearing today? Was Reilly watching us from afar, like I was watching him? Oh my gosh! He had memorized our outfits??!!

"Erm, excuse me?" a very familiar voice said.

I looked up from the table. And saw a MATH = EXCITEMENT SQUARED T-shirt.

Oh. It was Emma. My excitement plummeted. That's how Reilly knew. Emma was here in front of him.

"Hey, Emma." Nick knew her from homeroom.

"Excuse me," she said. "I need to borrow my sister."

"Can it wait?" I forced a smile and tried to communicate through twin telepathy. *Not now, I'm talking to Reilly. Not now—*

"Now," she said to me.

Emma and I needed to practice our twin telepathy.

"Later," I was about to tell her, when I looked at her closely. She was chewing on her hair and breathing kind of gaspy. Uh-oh. Something was wrong.

And that's when I realized she wasn't alone.

And so did Sydney.

"Ooh! Goody!" Sydney interrupted, clapping her hands in mock delight. "The Munchkins have arrived! Do you boys represent The Lollipop Kids?"

Mason and Jason were walking up to us, wearing identical plaid button-down shirts and khaki shorts.

"No," said Jason. "We represent the Case-Babbitt family."

"Are you a model?" Mason asked, staring wide-eyed at Sydney.

Sydney gave a smug smile.

Yikes. Time for damage control.

"We'll be right back," I said to everyone. I got up out of my chair and followed Emma and the boys over to the magazine section.

"Payton!" Emma said, in a fake cheery voice. "Remember how we told Counselor Case we thought the twins would benefit from some individual attention? And how you could spend some time with Jason?"

"Um, yeah," I said. "But not today."

"It turns out it *is* today!" Emma said, continuing the fake cheerful voice. "Mathletes was cancelled today, so Counselor Case switched our tutoring days."

I looked at Mason and Jason standing there. Mason was yawning. Jason was smiling at me.

"I'm in Drama," I hissed at her.

"You promised," Emma hissed back. "Plus, Jason threatened to have a tantrum if he was stuck watching 'baby math' and then Mason smacked him so Jason started hyperventilating and how would that look for us if my tutoring service project freaked out around your drama service project?"

Jason started sniffling.

I sneaked a peek over at the Drama table. A tantruming twin *would* be totally embarrassing.

"Payton!" Jason whined. "My mom said you're in Drama Club. Can you show me the tech stuff? The sound effects and the lighting? Pleasssse?"

"Pleasssse?" Emma asked at the same time.

"I told my mom you would today!" Jason announced. "I told her I'd behave as usual if you took me."

I had no choice and Emma knew it.

"Bye, Jason! And oh—you have the gecko, right?" Emma asked him.

"I got it." Jason pulled back his sleeve to show the reptile clinging to him.

Oh, Emma was tricky. She got rid of one twin nightmare and her gecko nightmare at the same time.

"Okay, I'll be with Mason on the other side of the library as far away as possible," Emma said, obviously trying not to panic at the sight of the gecko.

"Emma, text me when I need to meet you," I said.

I heard Emma breathe a huge sigh of relief as she walked away with Mason.

I looked at Jason. I looked at the table of Drama people, rehearsing their lines. Great. Just great.

Emma

Ten

THE LIBRARY

"Okay, Mason," I said. "Today we're learning about fractions." I took out a paper plate and a turquoise pen from my backpack.

"Imagine this plate is a pizza," I said in my best tutor voice. "How many slices would you want to eat?"

"None." Mason sneezed. "I'm lactose intolerant."

Then he sneezed again, blowing the paper plate off the table.

"Mason!" I said. "Please cover your mouth with your arm when you sneeze." I demonstrated, bending my arm and covering my nose and mouth.

"Oh, how sweet," said a voice behind me. "Emma is playing peek-a-boo."

I put my arm down and grimaced. Jazmine James. I swiveled around in my chair.

"Peek-a-boo, we see you!" Hector cackled. He was standing, as usual, a bit behind Jazmine.

"No," I said, trying to maintain my dignity while picking up the paper plate from the floor. "We are learning fractions."

"Oh." Jazmine smiled patronizingly. "That's good. Knowing fractions will help you in honors math, Emma."

"No," Mason explained. "*Emma* already knows fractions. She's teaching them to *me*."

"Yeah, she knows that. She was trying to be funny," I told him. "Obviously she failed."

"Fractions," Jazmine said. "Like you and your sister are one-half of a whole person? Or as in, 'If Emma gets a much, much smaller fraction of the math problems correct, then Jazmine will win the mathletes competition'?"

"Hey," Mason said. "Nobody disses my tutor. You're going down at the competition. Down."

"Down, boy." Hector cracked up. "Sit, stay."

"Jazmine, why don't you just ride your broomstick over to wherever it was you were going." I sighed. "And take your Flying Monkey sidekick with you."

But Jazmine was ignoring me. She'd grabbed the paper plate and blue pen and was writing something.

"Here are the odds of you beating me at mathletes, Emma," Jazmine said, leaning over to push the plate at me. Her smug face was right at Mason's level.

And then he sneezed. A big, wet sneeze.

"Ahhh! Ewww!" Jazmine jumped back, wiping her face frantically.

"I told you to cover your mouth when you did that," I told Mason mildly.

"Ooopsie, I forgot," Mason said. "Sorry!"

He didn't look too sorry.

"Hector, get me some tissues," Jazmine shrieked. "And stop laughing. Where's my hand sanitizer?"

"Excuse me, but you're disturbing the other students," Mrs. Nicely, the library media specialist, said, hurrying over to Jazmine. "I'll have to ask you to leave."

"But I have a book to get," Jazmine protested as Mrs. Nicely led her away.

Hector followed Jazmine out of the library.

It was quiet for a moment.

It was time to be a good role model and stick to the program. Be serious, Emma, mature.

"Did you know that a sneeze can reach speeds of one hundred fifty-seven miles per hour?" I asked him.

Then Mason and I cracked up, hiding our laughter behind our hands so we wouldn't be too loud. After we'd calmed down, I picked up the paper plate to teach fractions. And I saw:

$$1/1,000,000$$

Ugh. Jazmine had written the "odds of Emma beating me" as one in a million. I turned the plate over and reached into my bag. Fortunately, I'd brought extras. So then I demonstrated different fractions and their equivalents to Mason, who was comprehending the lesson remarkably well.

"So 4/8 equals 8/16," he was saying, when my cell phone rang.

Oops. I'd neglected to turn it off. I peeked at it. A text from Ox!!!

Yes. Yup. Affirmative.

"Very, very good, Mason," I said, reaching for my phone. Boy, I'm a good tutor, he's learning so quickly. "Now try equivalent fractions for one-third."

Ox's text said:

f-ball done. Can I c u?

I texted back:

Ok. Come 2 library.

What was I doing? I was supposed to be concentrating on tutoring, not socializing! But oh well, Ox was on his way! I reached into the little zippered pocket inside my bag and pulled out a lip gloss and little mirror, carefully, so Mason couldn't see what I was doing. I put the lip gloss up to my mouth and peered in the mirror. In the reflection, beyond my face, I noticed Mason was not looking at the paper plate or his scrap paper. I angled the mirror and saw he had something on his lap. He was tapping on it.

"Mason!" I said.

He jumped.

"What do you have there?"

"Um," he said. "One-third equals two-sixths, equals .333, repeating 3," he said quickly.

"No," I said, getting up and moving around to his side of the table. "What do you have *there?*"

"A calculator?" Mason said.

I took it from him. "Wait," I said. "This is a scientific calculator. Since when do you carry a scientific calculator? And wait a minute, since when do you know decimals? Point three repeating three . . . ?

Mason slouched in his seat.

"You're not Mason," I groaned. "You're . . ."

"Emma!" Ox walked up to our table.

For a moment my mind went blank. Mason and Jason *who?*

"Hi, Ox," I said. He looked good, as usual. A little rumpled from football and wearing his jersey over jeans.

"You're number 17," the twin's voice piped up. "Did you know seventeen is a prime number and chlorine is number 17 in the periodic table in a group known as halogens?"

"Ox, meet *JASON*." I sighed. Jason looked at me like, *Uh-oh, busted.*

"Ox, if you'll excuse us for just a moment?" I asked.

"Sure," Ox said, and went over to the magazines and picked one up.

"I cannot believe you'd do this, after we talked about how wrong it was," I said to Jason.

"I just wanted to do math with an intellectual person for

a change," Jason whined. "You wouldn't believe the kids in elementary school. They have no passion for higher math."

I couldn't help but be a bit flattered.

"Plus, Mason said he'd beat me up if I didn't do it," Jason added.

"Okay, kid, this way." I steered him in the direction of the Drama table, where I'd last seen Payton and the other twin heading. We passed Ox on the way.

"I'm sorry, Ox," I said. "I have to go."

"Uh. Um," he said. He was kind of bouncing a little and clearing his throat. Was Ox nervous?

"Emma," Ox said. "Some of us are going out for pizza after mathletes. Want to come with me? I mean, with us?"

Yes. Yup. Affirmative.

"That sounds great," I said, trying to sound calm and cool. "I'll have to ask my parents and get back to you."

"Great!" Ox smiled. "Great. Okay. See you."

As he walked one way toward the exit, I gripped Jason's shoulder and walked the other way toward the Drama table.

"Emma and Ox sitting in a—," Jason began singing.

"Quiet," I ordered. "You do not need to be in any more trouble than you already are."

Jason stopped singing.

We approached the Drama Club table and I saw Tess and (*ugh*) Sydney, and Payton's crush . . . but, what? No Payton. And no Mason! I had one twin and one missing twin! Where could Payton have taken him? I had no idea.

Eleven

LIBRARY

"So, Jason," I said. "I have an idea. Let's go hang out in a very quiet place in the library away from everyone and read books. I'm sure your gecko would like some peace and quiet."

"No way," Jason said. "My mom said I could hang out with the Drama Club. She said there's a boy who does special effects, like making sound effects."

"Well," I said, waving at my Drama friends who were rehearsing at the table. "The Drama Club is very busy right now."

"My mom *promised*," Jason said, and took off toward the Drama table. Crud.

I ran after him.

"Hi, Drama Clubbers!" Jason was saying as I reached them. He pulled out my former chair and sat down.

Everyone looked confused.

"Sorry," I said, trying to stay calm. "Um, this is Jason Case-Babbitt. His mom is Counselor Case. And his dad is Mr. Babbitt, the math teacher."

"Your dad is the mathletes coach?" Tess asked. "That's neat."

"Jason is great at math," I said. "But he's also interested in drama, so his mom said he could join us today."

"What are we, day care?" Sydney muttered.

"Sure, buddy." Nick smiled at Jason. "We're doing *Wizard of Oz*."

"Cool!" Jason said. "I love when The Flying Monkeys carry Dorothy away. They're like—"

Jason pushed his chair back and jumped up. He started racing around the table flapping his arms.

"Hello, Payton?" Sydney said, annoyed. "We're trying to rehearse here."

My face turned beet red. I couldn't even look at Reilly.

"Jason's usually the well-behaved twin," I said. "So, Jason, if you're going to stay you have to sit down quietly."

"Gotcha." He saluted me and sat down at the table. "How 'bout if I play with my Gameguy?"

He pulled his sleeve up. I saw a green tail flick.

Sydney furrowed her brow and leaned closer.

"Oh, wrong arm!" Jason said, and pulled that sleeve down, covering the gecko. Phew. He reached into his other sleeve. "This is where I hide my Gameguy!"

I wasn't sure that playing his handheld game was what his

mother would want. But it would keep him quiet while we rehearsed, right? Emma told me Jason was really into school-work, so it was probably a math game or something. Jason plugged in earphones and zoned out.

"We're on page 24," Tess said to me, and smiled. "Payton, can you read The Tin Man's lines? Charlie isn't here to be The Tin Man."

"I'm subbing for the Lion," Sydney announced. "Since Glinda isn't in this scene. It would be cool if she were, though. I could come down all beautiful and sparkling and dance across the Yellow Brick Road. . . ."

As Sydney tried to insert herself into every scene in the play, I listened as everyone read their lines. And then I jumped in with mine. It was fun being part of the reading. I tried to do my best Tin Man imitation.

"Oh, wait," Reilly said, slapping his head. "I lost my spot. Where was I?"

I repeated his last line, which I remembered because of the way he had said it—really cutely. *Ah.*

"Dude, I wish I could remember lines like that," Reilly said. "I'm going to be memorizing these lines for a year."

He looked so frustrated.

"Read them over and over out loud," I suggested. "Record yourself on your MP3 and listen to it over and over. Walk around and see if that helps you memorize."

Everyone looked at me.

"Um," I said, kind of embarrassed. "My sister, Emma,

taught me that so I'd stop bombing my history tests and stuff."

"Emma is so smart," Tess said.

"So, like before you were born, do you think she sucked up all the genes of genius, leaving you with none?" Sydney asked me.

Nick stuck up for me. "Payton's not dumb."

"No offense, Payton. I didn't mean it like *that,*" Sydney said, innocently, even though she totally did. "Just that, you know, it's weird how twins are so alike but so different."

"Yeah, that's true," Tess agreed. "Especially identical twins. Do you like being a twin?"

I was used to this. Twins get the questions about being a twin all the time.

"Well." I shrugged. "I don't know what it's like not to have a twin. But really, it's pretty cool. When Emma's not being annoying."

"And when she's not dressing in things like that T-shirt she was wearing today," Sydney said.

"Oh, our mathletes T-shirt?" Tess turned to Sydney. "I helped design that! Isn't it funny?"

Heh. Sydney was at a loss for words.

"Speaking of clothes, did your mom ever dress you guys alike?" Tess asked.

"When we were little," I admitted.

I shuddered at the memory of some of our baby pictures. Now our parents are really into letting us have "our own identities," and since we're so different, it isn't a problem. But when we were little, my mom did go through the dress-alike phase.

The problem was when we were babies you couldn't tell us apart. Later, we would argue over who was who.

"I'm the one smiling adorably," Emma would say. "You're the one eating her toenails."

"No, that's you," I would fight back. "And in the other picture where one of us is flashing her diaper? That's you, not me."

But after the baby times, we pretty much always dressed differently. And obviously, you could totally tell our clothes apart now. That is, when we weren't switching in the JC.

"Payton, when you guys were little, did you have a secret language?" Reilly asked me. Reilly smiled at me and—*ahhhh!*—his blue eyes crinkled! His perfectly white teeth shone like a spotlight!

He looked at me like *we* were sharing a secret language. A secret language of romance!

"Hello? Earth to Payton?" Sydney's irritating voice snapped me back to reality.

"Oh." I turned right. "Not really a secret language. Well, some words that we made up and didn't tell anyone about."

"Me and my brother have a secret language, too!" someone said loudly. It was Jason, who had taken out his earphones and was leaning forward.

"What does it sound like?" Nick asked him.

"'Blurp!' means 'Watch out, our mom is coming,'" Jason said. "'Floop! Floop!' means 'Dad's coming.'"

Everyone cracked up.

"And we have nicknames for each other," he said. "I'm Booger and he's Butthead."

"Nice." Reilly laughed. "Hey, Payton, do you guys have twin nicknames?"

"Yeah," I said, without thinking. "I used to call Emma MeeMa."

Everyone cracked up. It had been pretty funny. I'd called Emma that until kindergarten when, well, people made fun of us for it.

"What did Emma call you?" Nick asked.

"Wait, wait, let me guess," Sydney said. "If Emma is MeeMa, you must have been . . . PeePa!"

"No, wait." Nick laughed. "I bet it was PeePee!"

Traitor.

"PeePee!" Jason laughed.

"It's *not* PeePee," I said loudly over everyone's laughter. "Or PeePa. Yeesh, it was PooPa!"

As soon as I said it, I realized that was a mistake. PooPa wasn't exactly a whole lot better.

"PooPa?" Sydney said. "That's perfect! We can nickname you Poopy from now on!"

Sydney gave her giggle, which was her way of saying to the boys that she was just kidding, even though I totally knew she was trying to get me. She was very good at playing innocent, while still crushing me like a little bug.

"Poopy!" Jason cackled. "Poooooopy!"

"Jason, remember we're in the library. So shhh," Tess said gently, saving me. Whew. Let's move on.

"I shoulda been twins," Reilly said. "No, I shoulda been quintuplets. Five Reillys would be awesome."

Ah. The girls all sighed happily, thinking of more Reillys.

"It must be freaky being a twin," Sydney said. "I'm glad there's only one me."

"So am I," I blurted out. Um, oops. "I mean, you're one of a kind!"

Everyone laughed. Sydney awkwardly laughed, too, but gave me the squinty evil eye. Uh-oh. She was going to crush me.

"Maybe we should go back to rehearsing," I stammered nervously. "I mean, you guys should practice. Um, not that you need a lot of practice. You're all good actors."

"You're good at acting, Payton," Sydney said. "Like you totally had everyone believing you were Emma when you guys traded places."

"I missed all that," Reilly said. "You acted like your sister?"

"Oh, yeah," Sydney said. "They switched places. Everyone totally thought they were each other."

"It was an emergency thing," I said. "We're not going to do it again. It was kind of a disaster."

"They got in so much trouble," Jason sang out. "Emma's punishment is she has to tutor my brother. And Payton's going to take me backstage today to show me the sound effects and stuff. Right, Payton?"

"Well, we're not really doing the backstage thing today," I said to him. "The janitor is fumigating."

"What?" he said, and his voice got louder. "But my mom *said*. She *said!*"

Yeesh! And he was the "smart, well-behaved" twin? This was not going to turn into a major tantrum, was it? No wonder Emma couldn't deal with both of them.

"Looks like Payton is going to get a Fail from Counselor Case." Sydney giggled to Reilly.

"Hey, Jason," Nick said. "I make some of the sound effects in the computer lab. Want to do that with me?"

"Yeah!" Jason jumped up.

"Well, you guys have a good reading," Nick said. "Jason, Payton, and I are taking off."

"Do you need me?" Tess asked.

"No, you need to rehearse," I said. "But thanks."

"Bye, Poopy!" Sydney waved as she moved her chair closer to Reilly.

Grrrr.

I picked up Jason's Gameguy and followed Nick and Jason out the library door.

"What sound effects do you make?" Jason asked him.

"Storm and wind sounds when Dorothy gets stuck in the tornado. That one's pretty intense," Nick said. "I'm working on a lion roar for The Cowardly Lion at the end. It's going to be so loud it echoes."

"Sweet!" Jason said.

They talked nonstop as they walked down the halls and into the computer lab. Nick turned on a computer and we all pulled up chairs. I watched as Nick showed Jason how to find sounds and morph them in different ways. Jason was totally into it.

"Here, you make your own sound," Nick said to him.

"Thanks," I whispered to Nick as we watched Jason pressing buttons. "You saved the day."

"No problem," Nick whispered back. "Hey, I'm just glad someone appreciates the tech stuff. Most people just want to be on the stage."

"Yeah," I said. "I never really thought about the backstage stuff. Or the underneath-the-stage stuff. I'm an expert on that part, now."

"Maybe you'll get off early for good behavior," Nick said.

"I hope." I sighed.

"Until then, behind-the-scenes people rock," Nick said, and held up his hand. We high-fived.

"Attention! Attention!" Jason announced. "Presenting . . . my sound effect."

He raised the volume and hit a key.

Ppppffffffft.

The computer made a loud and disgusting fart sound.

"You made a fart?" I asked him.

"Yeah, isn't it awesome?" Jason asked. He hit the button again. *Pfffffft.*

Nick and I looked at each other and started laughing.

"I'll save that one," Nick said. "Maybe we can use that some-day."

"No way!" Jason said gleefully. He looked at me. "I know you're all grossed out at what I made."

"Actually, I see the possibilities," I said thoughtfully. "Like if someone acted like a diva onstage, then you could set off your sound effect . . ."

I leaned over and clicked the key a couple times.

Pfffffft. Pfffffft.

I pictured Sydney prancing onstage dressed as Glinda and then a fart noise going off. Heh.

I snorted.

"You're pretty cool!" Jason looked at me admiringly. "Your sister would have been mad at me, I bet. She'd be all, *that's gross and inappropriate.*"

"Yeah," I agreed. "She would. And she'd be right. But it's still kind of funny. What if you did a fart remix?"

Nick leaned over and taught us how to make a fart remix. We were laughing hysterically when—*Wham!*—all of a sudden the computer lab door slammed open. I spun around in my seat.

Emma was standing there, holding Mason by the arm.

"Confess!" she commanded.

"Um," I said. "It was just a fart noise. We were having a little fun!"

"NOT the fart noise," she said, and marched over with Mason in tow. She leaned down to look at Jason. "Confess!"

"Uh-oh," Jason said.

"We're busted," Mason said, and nodded.

Busted? Nick and I looked at each other.

"THAT"—Emma pointed at Jason, sitting in Nick's computer chair—"is not Jason. That is Mason. Isn't it? Confess! You traded places! I realized it when JASON was having an intelligent conversation with Ox!"

"Ooh!" I squealed. "You talked to Ox?"

Emma shot me a look. Oh, yeah, she should tell me about that later.

"Okay, okay," Mason—formerly-known-to-me-as-Jason—said, slumping in his computer chair next to me. "We confess. We switched."

"Why'd you guys switch?" Nick asked.

"I hate math," Mason said. "And I wanted to do the Drama Club stuff."

"And I love math," Jason said. "Although we had to do fractions today. Yeesh, I learned fractions when I was four. Baby stuff."

"Are you saying I'm dumb?" Mason leaned forward from his computer chair.

"Maybe," Jason said.

"Yeah, well this is way cooler than your stupid math!" Mason turned to the computer keyboard.

Pfffft. Pfffft.

"What was that?" Emma looked repulsed.

"My fart sound effect," Mason said proudly.

"That IS cool," Jason said admiringly.

❀ 119 ❀

"You spent the tutoring session teaching him to make fart noises?" Emma turned to me and glared.

"Hey!" I said. "I'm watching him to *help* you! YOU'RE supposed to be the tutor, not me."

"Heh, Emma, I made this sound effect just for you." Mason laughed. "You're our tutor. Get it? TOOTer. A fart? A TOOT!"

Pfffft.

"Did you know," said Jason, "that the speed of the gasses in a fart can reach twenty miles per hour?"

He and Mason cracked up. I bit my lip and looked over at Nick, who also was trying not to laugh.

"I've lost control." Emma put her face in her hands.

Pfffft. Pfffft. Pfffft.

I snorted. But that's when I saw it. The gecko was crawling out of Jason's—no, wait—*Mason's* sleeve.

"Oh, look," I said, pointing to the clock. "It's time to return the boys to Counselor Case. I'll walk you down, Emma."

That way I could distract her from remembering the gecko.

"Okay," Emma said weakly.

"Thanks for your help, Nick," I said to him. "That was, strangely, fun."

"No prob." He waved. "See ya, Jason and Mason. Whichever you are."

The four of us walked out of the computer lab.

"Don't explode," I whispered to Emma. "Let's just return them to their mother and not say anything about switching."

"We can't do that," she whispered back. "You have to tell your mother about the switch, boys," Emma said. "It's important to be honest."

"Okay," Mason said. "I can't wait to tell her about the fart noise Payton taught me."

"You can't," Jason said. "We'll get in trouble. I'll have to pretend I made the fart noise. You'll have to pretend you learned fractions. She'll probably quiz you on them, though. And you won't know anything. Mom will be pretty mad."

"Wait!" Emma said. "Um, maybe we shouldn't say anything to your mother. Just this one time."

The boys grinned at each other.

"We'll just tell Mom what great tutors you twins were," Jason said cheerfully.

"Toooot," Mason said. And made a noise.

Pffffft.

Emma

Twelve

DINNER AT CHINESE RESTAURANT

"So," my father said, picking up his chopsticks. "Tell us about your week so far."

"I went to school," Payton said, sipping a glass of water. "And then community service."

Payton and I had agreed beforehand not to mention the tutoring or tooting fiasco.

"I went to school," I echoed my sister. "And then to community service."

I maneuvered my fried dumpling into my mouth without dropping it. It had taken me four years of weekly family dinners at Blossom Chan's Chinese Restaurant to master the art of chopsticking.

Unfortunately, both Payton and I had inherited a klutz gene that made physical coordination difficult. Which is why we didn't play sports, unless forced to. It's also why

Payton was using her fork on her lo mein noodles. . . .

There was silence at the table. Except for some chewing noises.

"Well, I finished editing my magazine article on gardening trends," my mother said brightly.

"That's great, hon," my father said. "I had a successful day also. I sold out of umbilical cord clamps!"

I saw my sister's fork stop, with one long noodle dangling.

"Ewwww," Payton and I both said, completely grossed out.

"What?" my dad said, looking innocent. "I'm in medical supply sales. I sell medical supplies. And if you two girls aren't going to share the details of your day, then your mother and I will."

"Okay, we get your point," Payton said.

I kept eating. I wasn't going to let my parents off that easily. I was still sulking.

They had said "no" when I asked them if I could go out for pizza with Ox after mathletes. ("No, Emma, you can't go out with a group of kids we don't know. And we're already allowing you to socialize with your new friend Quinn. That's enough social life for now. You are still working on earning our trust.")

Excuse me, but perhaps I was making up for lost time since I never had friends before?

Or . . . a boyfriend.

Not that Ox was my boyfriend, since we were clearly not romantic or anything. But if he asked me to be his girlfriend . . . ?
I sighed.

Plop! My dumpling slipped out of my chopsticks into the bowl of Blossom Chan's special dipping sauce. Special dipping sauce splattered in all directions.

"Aaack!" . . . "Emma!" . . . "Be careful!" my family members said as they tried to dodge the mess.

I was unable to move away quickly enough and got the full force of fluid in my face.

"Trying out the special dipping sauce?" I heard a voice say as I wiped my face with my napkin. It was an evil voice.

"Or should I say *dripping* sauce?" the voice continued.

I glared up at Jazmine James.

"Just a joke, Emma." Jazmine laughed.

Oh. Ha. I forgot to laugh.

Unfortunately, my parents didn't. They actually thought it was funny.

"Hi, Payton," Jazmine said. "Hi, Mr. and Mrs. Mills. I believe you've already met my parents at academic events?"

Mr. and Mrs. James, looking as if they'd stepped out of a glamour magazine, said hello.

"Sit still, Emma," Jazmine said. "I'll get you more napkins. *Fúwùyuáh!*" she called out to our waitress. And then said something else in what sounded like Chinese.

Our waitress nodded and rushed over with extra napkins.

"Xie xie," Jazmine said.

"That means 'thank you,'" I told Payton.

"Oh, you know Mandarin Chinese also?" Mrs. James

asked me, one perfectly shaped eyebrow raised. "Our Jazmine is fluent in four languages; she has such a good memory."

Uh-oh. I only knew three words in Chinese: *xie xie,* pronounced "sheh sheh." And *ni hao* was "hello." I'd learned them one day last spring when I was home sick. I'd surfed to a public broadcasting animated kids' show. Apparently, learning Mandarin Chinese was big stuff in the preschool world. Oh, my third word was *dàxiàng.* The cartoon girl was looking for her lost friend, Daxiang the elephant.

Oops. I'd spaced out. All three Jameses were looking at me. Must. Impress. Them.

"Oh. Yes," I said wisely. "To be successful in competitions like Jazmine and I, you need a memory like a *dàxiàng.*"

Silence.

"You know—an elephant?" I persisted. "Because an elephant never forgets?"

Okay, nobody seemed too impressed. I picked up my water glass and drank.

"So, Mr. James, Mrs. James, what is it that you two do?" My father, the extrovert salesman, always tried to make conversation with anyone. Anyone. Even my mortal enemy???

"Stop!" I screamed. *"Do not engage with the evil ones!"* Actually, I didn't scream this out loud. Just inside my head.

My damp, spicy-sesame-sauce-dripping head.

My father was now in a discussion with the parents of the girl who had almost destroyed both Payton and me!

"Traitor," I mouthed to Payton.

"Clueless," she mouthed back, rolling her eyes.

I saw Jazmine squinting at us, trying to figure out what we were saying.

"Payton and I are fluent in a secret twin language," I said. "It's even more complex than Mandarin—you wouldn't understand."

"Womashukiloo," I mouthed, and nodded toward Jazmine. Payton mumbled some nonsense syllables back to me as well and we laughed.

Now Jazmine looked totally paranoid.

"Mother, Papa, I believe our table is ready," she said, and practically dragged her parents away from ours.

My twin and I watched as the James family was seated on the far side of the restaurant from us.

"She deserved it," Payton said, giving me a high-five.

"Yeah, don't mess with the Mills twins," I said. "Ever. Again." I was feeling totally twin-bonded with Payton.

"Ahem," my father said, clearing his throat. "I heard that, and I'd like to remind you that you two girls were in the wrong. When your friend caught you switching places, you were breaking the rules. She just brought it to your school's attention."

"Dad," I protested. "One, Jazmine James is not our friend. . . ."

"And, two," Payton continued, "she didn't have to humiliate us in front of the whole school."

❀ 116 ❀

Wow. We were really twinning out, completing each other's sentences.

"The girls have a point," my mother said, slurping her tea.

"Well," my father said. "Her parents were interesting. Did you know that Jazmine's mother has a novel that's going to be published this spring? It's titled, *Genius in my Family*."

Gag! I made that noise in my head, but my mother? She really gagged. Tea spurted out her nose.

My mother's dream has always been to write a novel. She has been working on one ever since I can remember. But it's still on her computer. Jazmine's mother's novel will be in bookstores and libraries.

Mrs. James: 1, Mom: 0

I would *have* to beat Jazmine in a competition soon. The James family must learn that the Mills are a force to be reckoned with.

Brrrrrp. It was a belch heard round the restaurant.

"Dad!" Payton and I groaned.

Okay, *some* members of the Mills family are a force to be reckoned with.

Our empty plates were swooped away by the waitstaff and replaced by fortune cookies. Of course, as a scientist, I did not put any credence in fortunes. But per family tradition, I broke into mine:

You are a winner through and through.
Lucky numbers: 4 and 7!

Well.

Perhaps I could believe a *little* in fortunes. I crunched on the cookie.

Payton read hers out loud. "'You will need to get on top of a situation quickly.' What does that mean? That's not a fun fortune." She crumpled it up. I tucked mine in my lemon-colored hoodie pocket.

My mom paid the bill, Dad left the tip, and our weekly dinner out was over.

When we were all in the minivan on the way home, my father said from the driver's seat, "Emma? Payton? Do you have a lot of homework tonight?"

Oh! Yes! I still had homework to do tonight. Well, no worries. I would whiz through it like I always did.

We pulled into our driveway. Home sweet home.

One hour later . . .

Homework, stupid homework!

I could not believe it. I had left my homework assignment folder *and* a book I needed back at school. In my locker.

I couldn't do my homework!!!!!

"Emma, why are you hyperventilating?" Payton asked as she walked into our bedroom. She saw me sitting on my bed trying not to freak out.

❀ 118 ❀

"My homework," I gasped. "I don't have my homework."

"Um." Payton just stood there. Then she called, "Mom? Dad?"

Nooooo! Not my parents! I lost it.

"Emma, honey, what's wrong?" Mom sat next to me on the bed.

"I . . . forgot . . . to . . . ," I sobbed.

"Oh, for—Emma left her homework at school," Payton finished for me. "Okay, that's not normal for *her,* but it happens to everyone else."

"Emma, it's okay," my mother said and patted my back.

My sobs lessened to sniffs. "Tom? Tissue, please?"

My dad had been standing there watching me melt down. Was he furious? Would he punish me? Would he yell that I was a screwup?

"Blow," Dad said, holding the tissue to my nose as if I were a little kid.

"Everyone has trouble adjusting to a new school," my father said. "I'm sure if you tell your teachers you'll make everything up over the weekend, they'll understand."

It wasn't only my homework. The twins tricking me. People confusing me. I felt like I'd lost control. I flopped back on my (signature color) turquoise bedspread.

"Tom?" my mother said, getting up. "I'm feeling a Wii bowling game coming on. Girls, interested in a game?"

"No, thanks," Payton said. "I just feel like chillaxing."

"I don't know what Payton just said, but I'm going to wind

down here," I told my parents. "But thanks for being so understanding. I promise it will never happen again."

"You know what's also never going to happen again?" my father asked. "A gutter ball. At least not by me. It's pins-only from now on!"

"Dream on," Mom said. As the family's undisputed Wii bowling champion, she said she had earned the right to trash talk.

They left, closing the bedroom door. I looked over at Payton. She had earbuds in, lying back on her (signature color) pink bedspread and was humming to some song.

Apparently that was "chillaxing."

I felt weird with no homework. But . . . there was always math! I picked up my mathletes competition handbook and opened it to Chapter 7.

Bzzzt. Someone was texting me! I looked over at my sister. It wasn't Payton!

Bummer about missing pizza. c ya at mathletes. Ox

"Payton!" I tossed my (blue) monster doll at her head.

"What?" Payton unplugged. "Are you still stressing about your homework? Don't kill my chill."

"I just got a text from Ox!" I told her.

My sister immediately jumped off her bed and came over to mine.

"Interpret this," I said, showing her my cell phone. "It's

❀ 120 ❀

a response to a message I sent earlier about having family obligations. Does he sound upset that I can't come? Does Ox think I don't want to go?"

"Hmm . . ." Payton wrinkled her forehead and said, "I think he's crushed! Devastated! He'll probably be too sad to even eat a slice!"

"You really should have a part in that play, Dramagirl." I rolled my eyes.

"Or maybe he's over it already," Payton said. "I overheard Sydney talking about going out for pizza. She'll cheer him up."

WHAT??? Slimy Sydney, who probably still wanted to steal Ox from me? Would she be able to get her revenge tomorrow??

"Aaaugh!" I shrieked.

"I'm kidding, I'm kidding!" Payton said. "Sorry. I guess it wasn't that funny."

"Yeah, I think you can go to chillax yourself now," I muttered.

"You don't chillax yourself," my twin said. "You just chillax."

Payton's grammar lessons always made so much sense. As I flopped back down on my bed, my mathletes workbook slipped off onto the floor. I didn't have the energy to pick it up. My mind was now swirling with thoughts of Ox (and another girl sharing a smoothie!). For once, there was just no room in my brain for work.

I fell asleep in my clothes, still thinking about boys and trendy fashion combinations, and zzzzz. . . .

Thirteen

FRIDAY LUNCHTIME

I bit into my granola bar as I opened my magazine to page 44 so I could take the quiz. Who would be my Celebrity Crush Match?

Would it be the shaggy-haired actor who made me laugh on my favorite comedy? The dark, brooding guy who made the perfect vampire in the movies? The pop singer? The rock star?

I took the last bite of my apple and tossed the core into the big trash can. I wasn't known for my aim and it hit the shelves instead. The shelves I'd been painting after school. I was in the stage basement. It was my new lunch hideout.

Why did I need a lunch hideout?

Because lunch was now my least favorite period of the day. My first couple days in middle school, lunch was my favorite period. I'd sat with Sydney, Cashmere, their friend Priya, and Quinn. But of course I wasn't going to sit with Sydney, Priya, and Cashmere anymore. And, sadly—well, for me, not for Quinn—Quinn's art teacher let her best students use the art studio during lunch period. So since I had nobody to sit with at lunch, I'd scoped out hiding places. This was my newest one. Other than the fact it was dirty, dark, and still smelled like the mop water Sydney had dumped on my head, it made the perfect alternative to the cafeteria for me.

I took a sip of my water and added up my results. A couple B's, A's, and C's and my Celebrity Crush Match is:

Mystery Man!—You didn't match perfectly with any of our four guys! Your match is still a mystery!

What? I didn't match with any of them? *Bluh.* I shut the magazine. I knew it was just a silly quiz, but it was annoying that I couldn't even get a crush match in a magazine—or real life.

I put the cap on my water bottle and tossed it at the trash can. It bounced off the can and rolled under the rack of costumes. I groaned and got up to retrieve it. I rolled the costume rack aside and sighed when I saw the beautiful pink long dress that Glinda, the Good Witch was going to wear. I'd been told that it had been used last year for the *Sleeping Beauty* play and the year before that for *Cinderella*, but it was still looking perfectly princessy.

I wondered what it would be like to wear it. I looked around and didn't hesitate. I pulled the dress off the rack and slid it on over my clothes. I swished over to the mirror and . . . *Ah.*

Princess Payton. I turned to admire myself. Yes, yes, I was no longer Cinderella cleaning the dungeon of the supply room. I was a princess! And, unlike the magazine quiz results claimed, I would have the perfect prince!

I closed my eyes and held out my arms like I was dancing with my perfect princely partner. . . .

I wondered who he would be! Was my perfect match in my school? It wasn't impossible! I mean, even my sister had Ox. Where was my perfect match? Where was he? I danced around, pretending I was in a fairy tale and that once I put on the magic princess dress my prince would appear to me!

"Hello?" The deep voice suddenly came out of nowhere. "Is someone down here?"

OH MY GOSH! OH MY GOSH! OH MY GOSH!

I stopped dancing. Was it magic? Was my perfect match, my prince, here for me?

"It's me!" I said. "It's me, Payton!"

A head stuck through the trapdoor in the ceiling. Who was it? It was . . .

The janitor.

"What are you doing down here? This is against school rules," he barked at me.

So not my magical prince.

"I'm sorry," I said. "I do my school service here! I'm not messing up anything! I'll leave!"

"You better," he grumbled. "Or I'll have to report you. And is that your costume for the play?"

"No," I said, looking down at the dress Sydney would wear.

"Then do not abuse the costumes," he grumbled.

And the trapdoor shut.

I sighed as I pulled the dress over my head and hung it back on the rack.

I tossed my magazine in my tote bag and the rest of my lunch in the trash. I climbed up the ladder and out of the theater, under the eye of the janitor.

As I went out into the hall I realized something else.

Not only did I not have a perfect match or a princess costume or a part in the play—I also didn't have a place to go. I had thirty-five minutes to kill before next period.

I thought about my options:

1) **Girls' bathroom**—I had done that before I discovered the stage basement. But teachers check there and kicked me out.
2) **At my locker**—I had done that before I discovered the stage basement. But teachers check there, too, and told me to stop hanging out in the halls.

Um.

Janitor's closet? But what if the janitor went there next?

Why couldn't I be an honors student like Emma and get to go to the library anytime I wanted to? (Well, for starters, I often forgot to turn in my homework and I didn't study on weekends. But that's another story.)

But wait!

I wasn't allowed in the library, but Emma was. I'd memorized Emma's schedule when we switched places, so I knew right now Emma was in Gym class! I could pretend to be Emma and sneak into the library!

Perfect plan. I didn't think the librarians would know the difference. There were like two thousand people in this middle school. But just in case, I Emmafied myself.

I pulled my hair up into a ponytail. I slouched over a little and did my best Emma imitation on my way down the hall to the library.

Don't mind me! I'm just Emma, the honors student, going to the library! I opened the library door and confidently walked in.

"Hello, Emma," a librarian said cheerfully.

"Um, hi!" I mumbled back. Figures, the librarian would know Emma. I bolted to one of the side tables, behind the row of vampire-themed books. Hmm. One of the books looked kind of interesting. I took it to the table with me for something to do.

Safe! I wasn't always the hugest reader, like Emma was. She read like a book a day. I was slower at it. But, this book looked better than math, so I opened it and started to read. And read. Ooh. It was good.

I totally lost myself in the book. I almost didn't hear the librarian across the room say, "Hi again, Emma."

Oh, Emma was here, too? I thought distractedly. Oh, no! Emma! Emma is in gym! I'm Emma!

I ducked behind a shelf of books and peeked around. It

was Emma and she had sat down at the table behind the encyclopedias! I whipped out my cell phone and texted her.

EMMA! Aren't u sposed 2 b in gym?

Brrzzzt!

I could hear Emma's phone buzz. I saw her pick it up and type back an answer.

Text message from Emma:

Yes, I am! What is up?

Emma might have the genius brain for the English language (and Chinese, Latin, and French), but she just could not do text right. I typed:

u mean sup?

Wait, *so* not important.

Y rnt u in gym?!?!

Emma texted back:

Got out of gym class. Told Coach I had phylangephlebitis. Really I have to do schoolwork. I am getting behind! So g2g study.

Then I saw her turn off her phone. WAIT! Oh, no! This was bad. I had to tell her I was pretending to be her. I looked around, trying to make an escape, but the librarian was sitting at her desk, guarding the door. Guarding against people like me who impersonated their honors student identical twin sister to sneak into her library!

Oh, no!

I couldn't just sit there, or the librarian might notice there were two Emmas in her library. I had to tell Emma.

I tossed my stuff into my tote bag, got down on my hands and knees on the floor, and started to crawl, hopefully unnoticed, behind the stacks of books closest to Emma.

"*Psst!*" I hissed. "Emma!"

Emma looked puzzled. She pulled out her cell phone and frowned.

"No! I'm not on the phone!" I hissed. "*Pssst!*"

Emma looked around but didn't see me. Augh. I reached into my tote bag and took out an eraser. I aimed and . . .

Score! It hit Emma in the leg! Now I'd gotten her attention!

"Ack!" Emma said.

Oh, no! Emma was totally freaking out! What the—?

"Emma!" I hissed, desperately.

Emma's eyes widened, and . . . she saw me!

Emma stood up and stomped over to my hiding spot behind a low shelf.

"*Shhh!*" I said. "I'm not supposed to be here."

"Obviously," Emma whispered, without looking down to give me away. Then she sighed. "I thought I was losing it. First I thought I was losing my mind and hearing voices. Then I thought the gecko was climbing my leg."

Wow. Emma really was kind of losing it.

"It was just an eraser," I said. "I wanted you to know I snuck in here."

Emma took a quick glance at me on the floor. Then she kicked me!

"Ow," I said. "What was that for?"

"Are you impersonating me without my permission?" she hissed. "You are! You're wearing a ponytail and I bet you're doing the hunched-over thing you claim I do! You're pretending to be me so you can get extra studying time in the library, aren't you?"

"NO!" I said. "I'm just trying to avoid the cafeteria."

"You can't just pretend to be me," Emma said. "I mean, look at this! Two Emmas in the same place. This is a fiasco."

"I'm sorry," I said. "But now how am I supposed to get out of here? I didn't know anyone would notice! I didn't know you were BFF with the librarians."

"Of course I am," Emma replied. "Library media specialists are a backbone of the school as well as a fount of knowledge."

"Swell," I said. "Just can you get me out of here without the fount seeing me?"

"Okay. Look, there's a bunch of people coming in," Emma said. "They're distracting the librarian showing their passes, so hurry up and walk right out. Just do *not* attract any notice."

"Okay," I said. "Thanks!"

I got up and adjusted my tote bag. I quickly hustled toward the door, and then gasped. The group of people walking in were people I knew.

Tess. Nick. Reilly. Charlie. Sydney.

My friends who were in the play. Plus Sydney. They all must have made a plan to rehearse together. Together. Without me. They didn't even invite me. They were just one happy group. Without me.

"Payton, flee!" Emma hissed at me.

I tried to blink back my tears and duck my head down so nobody would see me. I went past the librarian's desk, where she was checking my friends' passes. Safe! I pushed through the library door, and then—

MWONK! MWONK! MWONK!

The alarm went off! A light started flashing! Oh, crud! I'd put the vampire book in my bag and forgot to check it out!

The whole library turned to look at me. Sydney grinned. Emma groaned.

"Um," I said. "I'd like to check out a book?"

Emma

Fourteen

LOCKERS AFTER LAST PERIOD

"You look heinous," Payton said to me.

We were at our lockers after last period. Payton had Drama/school service today, and I had mathletes.

"Well, if you're going to impersonate me again without my knowing," I retorted, "you're going to have to make yourself look heinous, too."

I was grumpy. Very grumpy. I hadn't gotten much sleep the night before again.

"I said I was sorry and I'd never do it again," Payton whined. "Twinky swear." She held out her hand in our twin pinky promise. I was in no mood.

"And I thanked you a million times for pretending to the librarian that you'd asked me to come meet you to drop off your book," Payton continued.

Yeah. That book. Mrs. Nicely, the library media specialist,

had been a little suspicious when Payton claimed I had been reading about vampires in love, but she'd let it go. And as the custodian arrived to shut off the alarm, she'd let us go.

So, the double Emmas plus insomnia had made it a v-e-r-y long twenty-four hours.

Looking into my locker mirror, I scowled. Normally, my appearance was not a priority, but I was heading to mathletes. I needed to look alert, competitive, and fierce.

"Wait a sec," my twin said. "Here, a little concealer . . . some sparkle powder to make your skin glow. . . ." Payton patted and brushed things onto my face.

"Now, pinch your cheeks and flip your head to fluff your hair," Payton instructed.

I pinched. I flipped—my ponytail whapping me on my way back up. I looked into my mirror again.

"Better," I admitted. My insides were still droopy, but my outside looked fresh. I made my competition face. Oh, yeah. Fierce.

"You look good," Payton said. "Except that face you're making? It makes you look like you're in pain. Are you in pain?"

"No." I shut my locker and made my face look like normal. "Thanks for the makeup help."

"At least one of us *needs* to use makeup after school." Payton sighed.

Oh, yeah. Payton had to spend her time under a stage.

"It's just weird that it's *you*," she added.

We said bye to each other and headed off in different directions.

It was *weird* that I was the one who needed and wanted makeup. But lately a lot of things had been unusual. As I walked down the hallway, my backpack felt unusually heavy. I was tired. Which was *not* that abnormal. I had often stayed up late studying, memorizing, problem-solving, and preparing.

But last night? I went over to Quinn's and had a fun (fun!) time. Then the fun ended when I had to do my regular homework and my makeup work from the day before. (The teachers weren't fazed by my first-time lapse. They just said things like, *Don't make a habit of it.*)

Right. Like I would. I only had good habits, like study habits and hygiene habits and organization habits. Oh, and that chewing-on-my-hair-when-I-get-anxious habit. Well, nobody's perfect.

After being with Quinn, after double homework, I got to bed late. But I couldn't sleep. I had so much on my mind. Like Ox. Especially Ox. Did he like me? Did he *like* like me? Did I *like* like him? (Final answer: Yes.)

If I couldn't go out for pizza, would he lose interest in me? Would he notice that other girls were prettier, more fun, and girlier than I was?

Last night, as those totally unwanted thoughts raced around my head, I realized I could handle this situation like I always do. Research. Unfortunately, it was way past bedtime, and I couldn't turn on the computer. So I went over to Payton's (pink) side of the room and grabbed one of her few books. It had a smiling girl surrounded by both boys and girls. Okay, they were all ridiculously good-looking, but perhaps I could find some information on relationships.

By 3:00 in the morning I had read about:

- **Mean girls.**
  (I already knew Sydney and Jazmine, so that was not enlightening.)
- **A nice new girl who tried to fit in with the popular clique, only to realize that that wasn't what she truly wanted.**
  (Like Payton during the first few weeks of school. Again, not educational.)
- **Boys who mostly goofed around and made little contribution to society or to the girls.**
  (Unlike Ox, who supported animal causes and was nice to girls. Especially me.)

That book was not at all helpful (although it did give me a few cool ideas for some outfits to suggest to Quinn).

Yup. I was still clueless and now also exhausted. But when I reached the classroom where mathletes was held, it was like a burst of energy went through me. I walked through the door, head high, shoulders back, and took a seat.

Other students came in. I focused on laying out my materials. Mechanical pencils. Scientific calculator. Plenty of paper—ruled, blank, and graph. Finally, the mathletes handbook. There. I was ready.

"Hey, Emma," Ox said, sliding into the seat behind me. His long legs stuck out, one on either side of me. His sneakers were huge, compared to my feet. Which were also in sneakers under my desk. If I moved my foot about five inches, I'd be touching him.

"Emma?" Ox repeated.

"Oh, hi, Ox," I said. I turned around and smiled. "I was just focusing on math," I said.

"I guess I'd better focus, too." Ox smiled. "Being around you can get me a little distracted."

What did that mean? How could anyone translate this foreign language of flirting? Was he even flirting? Or was he literally just distracted? Did Ox have attention problems? Did I??? I was supposed to have my attention on numbers, not a boy!

Fortunately, Coach Babbitt walked into the room just then.

"Today's a big day for you middle-school mathletes," Coach Babbitt announced.

I spun around to face forward. Out of the corner of my eye I saw Jazmine James. I blinked her away, out of my vision.

Today was all about the math.

"We're going to have a simulation countdown round," Coach Babbitt said. "For those of you who are new, when we compete against other schools and homeschool teams there will first be a written exam. The Top 10 scorers of the written test will be called up onstage to face each other in a head-to-head challenge. The countdown round is live in front of an audience, and you've got to answer math problems correctly against an opponent. The winner of that pair will go up against the winner of another pair until we get down to the final two mathletes. One last round, and we'll have a winner!"

Adrenaline shot through me at the word "winner."

"Of course, you all can't participate today," the coach continued, "because we have twenty-two students in the club. So, I'm going to ask for volunteers. . . ."

Hands shot up. Mine was first.

"And, remember, if you don't get chosen, you'll have a chance next week. We'll have three more weeks after that until our first real regional competition."

Everyone cheered.

Someone yelled, "Go, Geckos!"

I looked around. Huh. Only about half the kids had their hands up.

"Of course, if you don't want to be up in front of the group, for whatever reason, you don't have to," Coach Babbitt said. "Being a mathlete means having fun with math, and if you're just here for the problem-solving and not for competition, that is absolutely okay."

I heard a few "phews" around me. I raised my hand higher. I was here for the fun of competition, to be in front of everyone and show them I am a winner!

Like last year's state spelling bee c-h-a-m-p-i-o-n.

Coach Babbitt was picking people with their hands raised, and—YES!!!—he pointed at me. I rushed to the front of the room.

Ten of us stood at the whiteboard. Each of us was given a

dry-erase marker. Mine was blue—almost my signature color! Surely that would bring me luck. *Not that I would need it,* I told myself, eyeing my competitors. They included Jazmine James, Hector, and . . . Ox. But right now, even Ox was just someone to be taken down. It wasn't personal. It was math.

The first two people Coach had called up listened to their math problem. *Squeak, squeak* went their markers on the board. The boy with the red marker got it right, but the girl with green was off by a lot. She shrugged and smiled and sat back down as everyone clapped.

Then it was *my* turn! (Okay, my partner's turn, too.) Coach Babbitt read the problem aloud, and *squeak, squeak,* my blue answer appeared on the whiteboard.

"Correct, Emma," Coach Babbitt said. "And also correct, Hector. You both stay."

Everyone clapped.

And so it went. Within ten minutes the problems had gotten much harder. There were only four of us left standing at the board. Besides *moi,* there was Paul, an eighth grader who was the best mathlete on last year's team (which wasn't very good—they didn't even make it to States).

So the three of us left were seventh graders: me, Jazmine, and . . . Ox. I looked over at him. He was looking at me! He was smiling at me! He was going head-to-head with Jazmine on a question! He was so cute!

And wrong. Ox was going back to his seat after a particularly difficult geometry problem. Jazmine had gotten it right.

Poor Ox, I thought. *Bad Jazmine.*

My turn. Up against Paul. We both got the next problem right. Paul versus Jazmine. Paul goofed. Jazmine got it.

It was down to two.

"Congratulations, Emma and Jazmine," Coach Babbitt said. "Regardless of which one of you wins, you both should be proud of yourselves."

Yeah. Sure. Proud. Not yet!!!

I looked over at Jazmine, who looked back at me. Game on.

First math problem. *Squeak, squeak* of markers. We both got it right.

Second math problem. No problem. We both got it right. Third . . .

"Hi, Emma!" I was startled out of my "math zone." Coming in the door were Counselor Case and her twins.

I waved at Mason and Jason, gritting my teeth into a fake smile.

"Two minutes until dismissal," Counselor Case said. "I'm sorry if we're interrupting. The boys and I will be quiet."

"We'll be quiet," Mason shouted.

"No problem, honey," Coach Babbitt said to his wife.

No problem? That *was* the problem—we needed the next math problem. I needed to . . . Take. Jazmine. Down.

Coach Babbitt read the next problem. I got it right. So did Jazmine.

The other mathletes started clapping for us.

Another problem.

Both right.

"One last problem," Coach said.

I took a deep, cleansing competition breath. Which turned into a yawn. A yawn?

If $1/x + x = 3$, what is the value of $1/x^4 + x^4$?

Squeak, squeak . . .

"Emma, I'm sorry but your answer is incorrect," Coach Babbitt said. "That makes Jazmine the winner today. Good job, everyone!"

I heard packing-up-and-getting-ready-to-leave noises from the seats. I looked at my blue answer: 49. Then I looked at Jazmine's answer. It was in hot pink, and it said 47. Forty-seven???

"Emma's number two!" Mason yelled. "Number two . . ."

And I heard the twins giggling.

"Get used to it, Mills," Jazmine said as she capped her pink marker and strutted back to her seat.

I put my marker down in the tray and walked back to my seat. I felt like I was moving in slow motion.

"You did great!" Ox said as I started packing my stuff.

Then some other people said nice things to me as they passed on their way out the door.

"Thanks," I managed to choke out.

Coach Babbitt saw me lose. Counselor Case saw me lose. Everyone important to my future saw me lose to Jazmine James.

I put on my hooded sweatshirt because at this hour it would

be chilly outside. I picked up my backpack and walked out of the mathletes room alone, because I needed to be by myself. I was in shock because I lost.

Cause and effect. I screwed up (cause) and Jazmine beat me (effect). As I walked through the hallways, I realized:

1) Instead of preparing for Math last night, I had
       been thinking about Ox and even about Quinn
       and fashion.
2) My feelings about my love (?) life and social life
       had given me a bad night's sleep.
3) Boys + friends = Losing competitions.
4) Emma = Loser.

I was outside, almost at the bus. I put my free hand in my hoodie pocket.

What's this?

I pulled out the fortune cookie fortune. I'd worn this lemon-yellow hoodie last night at the restaurant. I read the fortune again.

You are a winner through and through.
Lucky numbers: 4 and 7!

Four and seven? As in Jazmine's winning answer, 47? *Aughhh . . .*

I crumpled up the paper, shoved it back into my pocket, and got on the late bus.

I saw Payton and sat down next to her.

"Emma, what's wrong?" she asked me.

I just shook my head, unable to speak. Everything was becoming clear. I needed to change my equation.

$$0 \text{ boys} + 0 \text{ friends} = 0 \text{ distractions}$$
$$0 \text{ distractions} = 100\% \text{ focus} = \text{winning}$$

I sighed.

I needed to make some changes in my life.

I had to go back to being AcadEmma.

Fifteen

FRIDAY NIGHT

"AcadEmma?" I frowned. "What the heck is that?"

"It's a lemma," Emma told me, "to solve my dilemma."

"Why are you talking in riddles?" I asked. Emma was usually weird, but this was even weirder than usual.

We were in our family room, waiting for dinner. I was playing a game on my cell phone. Emma was lying on the couch. I'd thought she was sleeping. Maybe she was.

"Are you talking in your sleep?" I asked.

"No." Emma sat up. "I'm making total sense. A 'lemma' is an obvious statement, like 2 + 2 = 4. Archimedes was into lemmas. And my *dilemma* is how to get back into winning mode. So, the obvious solution is to become AcadEmma. All academics, all studying, all the time. Payton, I'm going back to my old self. Before middle school got in the way."

Hmmm. That sounded wrong to me, but maybe Emma

had a point. Emma had always had a place where she was comfortable. A place she fit in. Her brain.

But me? Today had been the perfect example of Payton fitting in nowhere. Of course, not at lunch. Or with frenemies.

Even my own locker wasn't "me" anymore.

Earlier that day, I had stopped off at my locker. (Okay, I didn't really *need* to, but that was one of the times I didn't really have any specific place to be but had some time to kill.) Anyway, I'd thought, I'd visit the happy little slice of middle school that was all mine.

I'd smiled a little, thinking about my so-cute beady curtains dangling down. I'd put up magnets and pictures of fashion bags stuck on with Sticky Tack. Okay, true, it had been getting a little messy lately but still. It was *my* mess.

I'd spun the lock, opened it up, and . . .

SHOCK! It was clean! And there was a turquoise Post-it note on my locker mirror.

Surprise! Your mess was driving me insane.
Please note I organized your books by class period,
so do not mess it up! –Your twin, Emma

"So what's up with *this*?" I asked Emma, holding up a turquoise sticky note.

"Oh, yeah." Emma squinted at it. "Don't you feel much better now?"

"Nooooo," I said slowly. "I do not feel better after somebody invaded my privacy and property."

"You could thank me," Emma said from the couch.

"Or I could be seriously annoyed at you," I said. "Acad-Emma."

"Thank you for reminding me," my sister said. "I have serious academia to get to."

And Emma left. After Emma left, I turned on the family room computer.

This past week of cleaning under the stage had exhausted me. Need. To. Zone. Out. I pulled up YouTube. Perfect.

I stayed there pretty much all weekend, taking breaks only to eat and sleep.

Sixteen

SATURDAY AND SUNDAY

Studying. Reading. Memorizing. Homework. Competition training. More studying. Eating. Sleeping. Studying.

My weekend was a total success.

I had no idea what Payton had done this weekend. I'd holed up in our bedroom, and she was somewhere else. Where? I didn't even have time to ask.

Seventeen

MONDAY AFTER SCHOOL

"Hi, Payton."

I had my head buried in my locker. I looked out to see Quinn waving.

"How was your weekend?" she asked.

"Great!" I fibbed. What was I supposed to say—*I watched too much YouTube and ate too many snacks?* The truth sounded depressing. The truth *was* depressing. Well, at least I'd caught up on my sleep.

"Great!" Quinn said back with a smile. "Have fun at Drama!"

"Thanks." I smiled back. *I'm such a faker. Fake. Faker.* It would be another day *underneath* the Wonderful World of Oz and all the fun people.

I put away my school stuff as the final dismissal bell rang. Time to go into extracurricular mode.

I shifted some books to the side and then realized something. Oh, no! I was supposed to go to my "slave shift" under the stage, but I'd forgotten to bring spare clothes. I looked down at my outfit.

- ☑ Silky pale green tank
  (Summer Slave clothes)
- ☑ White hoodie
  (An Emma-purchase during twin switch from the mall)
- ☑ My favorite skinny jeans

Some of my favorite clothes! Clothes that would be totally ruined under the stage! Destroyed!

I leaned against my locker and groaned. My clean, organized locker. I stood up straight as I realized something. Just like Emma had my locker combination, I had the combination to her locker. And Emma always had backup everything. Calculators, pencils, and . . . clothes! Emma-clothes, which meant that I wouldn't have to worry about getting them dirty!

If Emma could go into my locker without permission then it was my turn. (Okay, she was in mine to help me, and I was in hers to steal and ruin her clothes but . . . anyway.)

I twirled her lock and opened her locker. And there, shelved under the section "Miscellaneous" that she'd marked with her label maker, was a bag of clothes. Score! I looked inside. Apparently, I'd be wearing a CALCULUVS! shirt and some gray sweats. Whatever.

It wasn't like anyone saw me under the stage, I thought as I walked to the stage basement. Or heard me, or even pretty much knew I existed under there. Okay, yeah. I'd been feeling sorry for myself ever since I saw everyone from Drama getting together without me. Tess had told me that Mrs. Burkle had given them a pass to rehearse together.

I climbed down the ladder to the stage basement and looked around. Today I was supposed to organize five bajillion lightbulbs into the right boxes. Fun!

I could hear the play rehearsal start upstairs.

I heard Sydney say, "'I'm Glinda, the Good Witch of the North.'"

Tess, as Dorothy, was saying, "'But witches are old and ugly! You can't be a witch! I've never heard of a beautiful witch before, like you are.'"

Ugh, ugh. I should have brought my iPod so I could block out hearing Tess tell Sydney she was beautiful.

"'Oh, but only bad witches are ugly,'" Sydney said, reciting her line.

I know someone who is ugly on the *inside*, I thought bitterly. I put a lightbulb away so hard I broke it. Oops.

Okay, I needed to chill. I couldn't let my jealousy and leftoutedness turn me into a witch, too. I continued to listen to everyone reading their lines as I put lightbulbs into little boxes. I'd heard the play so many times now, I practically had it memorized. I started to recite the lines along with everyone.

"'We're off to see the Wizard!'" I sang along. "'The Wonderful Wizard of Oz!'"

Ah, it would be so fun to be an actress. As I boxed bulbs, I imagined being a famous actress onstage. I daydreamed about being in the play, and having someone discover me. Like, a talent scout from Broadway! (Okay, I can't really sing but in my daydreams I could.)

And the talent scout would come watch our school play and would make it a point to tell Mrs. Burkle that he had spotted the newest, hottest, undiscovered raw talent.

And Burkle would gasp and say, *"Who?"*

And the agent would say: *"Payton Mills!"*

"Payton! Payton Mills!"

I blinked myself out of my daydream. Because someone was really calling my name!

The trapdoor was open, and Zahra, the high school helper, peered in.

"Payton!" she said. "Mrs. Burkle said to tell you someone is here asking for you."

I had the sudden crazy thought that it was a Broadway talent scout. Of course, that couldn't be possible! I wasn't even onstage! But maybe it was someone exciting! I was slightly dazed as I climbed up the ladder to see who was here for me.

I climbed up onto the stage, and waiting for me backstage was—one of Emma's tutor twins. Oh. I slumped a little bit.

"Payton!" he said, running up to me.

"Jason? Mason?" I peered at him closely.

"Mason," he said. "Honest. I'll tell you a secret trick. I have a freckle on my belly and Jason doesn't."

He showed me, proudly.

"Mason." I sighed. "Am I supposed to babysit you again today?"

"Nope," he said. "Nick is! Nick said I could help him backstage with the lighting! I get to blink the lights on. And off. And on! And off—"

"I got it," I said. "Well, that's cool. Why did they call me?"

"I asked Burkle where you were," he said. "She said you were cleaning under the stage and then she asked me to get you. She says you're needed."

"Really? Is that true?" I asked him.

"Payton Mills, this way!" Burkle's voice boomed across the stage. "I need another live body to help out onstage today."

"I gotta go," Mason said. "Nick said I could help with props. I don't know what props are, but I'm gonna help!"

He went off one way, and I went off to see Mrs. Burkle.

"A couple of people had to leave early for choir, so you can help out in the show," Mrs. Burkle said.

Yay! Even if I was just filling in, it was still my stage debut! Unfortunately, I was wearing Emma's CALCULUVS! shirt and her sweats, but I wasn't going to complain! I followed Burkle onstage. There was Tess and . . . Ah. Reilly.

"Please go over by Reilly," Mrs. Burkle said.

"Hi, Payton," Reilly said.

Ahhhh. Starry-eyed, I went to stand near Reilly. I wondered what part I was going to be playing.

"Hmm. Payton, hold your arms out to the side," Mrs. Burkle said.

I held my hands out, like a scarecrow. But Reilly was playing The Scarecrow, so I still didn't know what I was doing.

"Nick, how does Payton look?" Mrs. Burkle called from offstage, where Nick and Mason were standing.

How did I look? I saw some of the cast in the audience seats start cracking up at that. I blushed. What was he supposed to say? *Fine? She's kinda cute?*

"Lopsided," Nick said.

WHAT?

People really laughed hard now.

"Her hand needs to be a little higher for the apples to go past without hitting," Nick said. He walked over and gestured for me to raise my right hand.

"Nick," I whispered. "What am I supposed to be?"

"The tree," he said. "There's a scene where a creepy tree throws apples at The Scarecrow, The Tin Man, and Dorothy when they're walking down the path to scare them away."

I'm a creepy tree?

"I'm making a tree with a device that throws apples," he said. "Don't worry, they're just plastic fake apples. We're working on stage props this week."

I'm not even a person? I'm a stage prop???

"Perfect!" Mrs. Burkle said. "Let's do the scene. Nick, just launch the apples for now until we get the real tree built."

They're launching apples at me? Nick and Mason went over to some lever/pulley thing.

"Okay, Mason," I heard Nick say. "When I say, launch . . ."

"Bombs away!" Mason clapped his hands, happily.

"Action!" Mrs. Burkle called out.

So I stood there like a tree as Tess, Reilly, and the boy playing The Tin Man walked up to me.

"'I think we're lost,'" said Tess/Dorothy.

"Launch!" I heard Nick whisper.

Suddenly a plastic apple flew over my shoulder and landed in front of Tess/Dorothy.

"'Who threw that?'" The Tin Man asked. "'Who-who's there?'"

They looked around dramatically.

"'That tree is really creepy,'" Reilly said, pointing to me.

Reilly just called me a creepy tree. This was humiliating. This was my stage debut? I slumped my shoulders in defeat. And then—

OW!

"Whoops!" Mason yelled. "You moved your arm! I didn't know you were going to move!"

The plastic apple that nailed me rolled noisily off the stage. People were roaring now.

"Payton, are you okay?" Mrs. Burkle asked. "I'm sorry, maybe that wasn't the best idea. Nick, move a chair over to where Payton's standing and use that as your tree. We'll just make do for now. Payton, I'm sorry to have called you up here. We're fine without you."

I was being replaced by a chair.

They were fine without me.

I went back to the basement, in utter defeat. I looked around. It looked as clean as my Emmafied locker. I had to admit, I made a good Drama slave—erm, school service worker. I'd swept, scrubbed, and decluttered. And the basement makeover was complete.

Now what?

I pulled out my cell phone and texted Emma.

Sup?

Emma's response:

J is ☹—Ugh. No gecko—☺

I texted:

M is here with Nick helping. I'm cleaning. ☹

I shouldn't be interrupting her tutoring, but it seemed like I hadn't talked to my twin in forever. She'd been buried in her studies. Emma would probably appreciate a break from all her seriousness.

How's Ox? I texted, figuring I'd bring a smiley to Emma's thoughts.

Ox who? Emma texted back.

What?

What? I texted.

G2G, Emma texted.

Perfect. Emma finally uses textspeak . . . to cut me off.

Ox who? What did she mean by that? Emma and I talked about everything—but she hadn't mentioned anything about Ox.

I sat down on a stool painted like a tree stump. (Sheesh, this Drama Club used a lot of trees in their plays.)

Then it hit me. Emma didn't want to talk/text about Ox, because . . . Ox BROKE UP WITH HER!!! Wait. They weren't officially going out. But it was still obvious that they liked each other. Or did.

Poor Emma.

Poor, heartbroken Emma.

I looked at the time and realized my shift was over. I should go to Emma, and help her through this traumatic time. I trudged across the basement and climbed the ladder. I thought about my sister's first boy crush crushing her heart. *Grr . . . boys.*

"Why are you looking at me like that?" Nick asked as I emerged from the underground and onto the stage.

Oops. I must've been looking angry.

Nick was moving the trees off the stage. Everyone else was

in the audience seats, while Burkle was passing out papers or something.

"Sorry," I said. "Not your fault."

"Sorry you got nailed with an apple," he said. "Mason and I felt bad about that."

"It's okay." I smiled at Nick. He was a nice boy.

"I know sometimes I would do something like that on purpose," Mason said to me. "Like if you were mean, it would have been kinda funny. *Bam! Splat!* Hit with an apple! But this time it was really an accident. Sorry."

"Apology accepted," I told him.

"Hey, nice shirt," Nick said.

I looked down and rolled my eyes. CALCULUVS!

"It's really Emma's," I explained. "Only my twin sister would advertise that calculus goes with . . . well, um . . . love."

I looked at Nick. Was it my imagination? Or were his cheeks turning pink? And why did my face feel hot?

"Hey, tech guy!"

Reilly came over. Now my face felt even hotter. Could this boy be any better looking?

"Could you adjust the lighting during my scenes?" Reilly asked Nick. "I think I'd look better with a bit more light."

"You're a scarecrow," Nick said. "You're supposed to look like you could scare away crows."

"Well, you can't see me enough," Reilly was saying.

"It's so true," Sydney cooed as she came over. "You can never see enough of you good-looking Drama boys."

She gave Reilly a flirtatious smile. Ugh.

"And that includes you, Nicky," Sydney said, turning to Nick. "I don't know why you want to be backstage. You could be an actor, too!"

Double ugh.

"Good thing he's backstage." I surprised myself by speaking up. "I mean, without Nick's tech stuff, the play wouldn't be nearly as good. Backstage is important, too!"

I had a moment of happy when I saw Nick smile at me, but it was soon eclipsed by Sydney's less genuine grin. Sydney moved over so she was standing next to me.

"Backstage *is* important," Sydney said loudly. Then, under her breath, so only I could hear her, she continued, "However, under the stage? So NOT important. A place to hide *loooosers*."

"But Payton's under the stage," Mason said, apparently also hearing her.

"Exactly," Sydney said to him.

Mason's eyes became slits and he walked away.

"Anyways, dude, work on that lighting," Reilly said to Nick.

"Ooh, and that gives me an idea," Sydney squealed. "I can put glitter face powder all over my face and then when the light hits me I'll sparkle! It will highlight my—OUCH!"

Sydney suddenly jumped and grabbed her butt. And something clattered across the stage. An . . . apple?

"What happened?" Reilly and Nick asked her.

"Something hit my butt!" she wailed.

Reilly snickered.

"I mean my *back*." Sydney looked embarrassed.

"Ooopsie!" a voice called from offstage.

We all turned to see Mason, next to the apple launcher, calling over. "I was just moving this and it accidentally went off. My bad!"

I tried to hide a grin behind my hand.

"I think I need to go supervise the props," Nick said, also looking like he was going to smile.

"Smile all you want," Sydney growled to me. "You won't be smiling when I'm onstage and you're underneath it."

Yeah, yeah. I know. Sydney could always get the last word. But at least she had to say that while rubbing her . . . back.

"Exit everyone!" Mrs. Burkle clapped her hands and shouted. "Shoo, people! Go home and practice your lines. We do not have much more rehearsal time until our performance!"

Everyone filed out of the auditorium, excitedly talking about the play. I sighed. There were different plays put on during each year, so the tryout-rehearsal-performance schedule took place over a few weeks. I would probably still be stuck doing school service when auditions for the NEXT play were held.

All this just because Emma and I had traded places.

Emma!

I just remembered. Ox! I picked up my pace and made it to the bus in time to save a seat for my sister. When she got on and sat down next to me, she looked miserable.

"Emma, if you want to talk about Ox I'm here for you," I said, quietly, so no one else could hear. Inside my head, though, I was screaming *Talk! Tell me what happened! I need details!*

But all Emma did was sigh, and then grumble, "Math and romance can *not* coexist."

Whew. Good thing I'd put a jacket over the borrowed T-shirt. CALCULUVS! was the last slogan she needed to see.

Eighteen

MONDAY AFTER SCHOOL

I was in full AcadEmma mode, and had gotten all my old habits back. At first it was tougher than I'd anticipated. While *I* knew my new equation (0% social + 100% academics = ME), other people did not.

Quinn had grabbed me earlier in the day in the halls between PE (waste of time) and Study Hall (best use of time). "Emma," she'd asked. "So when do you want to do something after school? This week?"

"Oh," I'd said, startled out of solving a math proof in my head. "Quinn. No. I mean, I can't. I've got too much work to do."

"Okay," Quinn said. "Next week?"

I'd looked at my newish friend. She was bouncy and fun, and it looked like she'd gotten her hair cut. I'd fought the urge to comment on it. No. My social life had to be ripped away like a Band-Aid. Fast and painful at first, but no nonsense. No second thoughts.

"Quinn." I took a deep breath. "I'm really trying to focus on my studies these days. You know, with the mathletes competition coming up; and then there's the Geobee and Scrabble-lympics not far behind. . . ."

My voice had trailed off as I watched Quinn's face go from smiling to not smiling.

"I understand," she said. "I really do. Good luck with all that. I just hoped—well, I had lots of fun with you that time you came over."

Quinn gave a little half wave and walked away.

I had fun, too! the voice in my head yelled after her. *Lots of fun!*

"Bad voice," I'd muttered. "Go away."

I heard some giggling. I looked. Yup. The girls were laughing at me, talking to myself.

I ignored them. Things were back to normal.

I had been polite but monosyllabic to anyone who had tried to engage me in conversation today. I was beginning to feel like I had my time and my brain to myself.

Except for one tiny exception.

"Hey, Emma."

Okay. Not so tiny. Very tall, actually.

"Uh—hi, Ox," I squeaked.

I was at my locker. I pretended to ponder which books to bring home. (The real answer? All of them.)

"What's going on?" Ox asked me.

"Oh, the usual," I replied, trying to stay cool.

"No," Ox said slowly. "I mean, what's really going on? You've been acting . . . distant. I thought we were going to go over some mathletes problems this weekend on iChat."

I had ignored his chat request.

"And you didn't answer my text," he finished.

I know. Sigh.

"Emma, did I do something wrong?"

Yes, I thought. *You distracted me.*

"No," I said. "Not at all. It's just that I'm really, really busy these days."

Even to me, that sounded weak.

"Okay," Ox said, after a moment. "It's just that maybe you should give someone a clue, before you blow them off. Instead of leaving them hanging."

Clangggg! Clanggg! The bell rang. Ox didn't move. I knew if I spoke I might break down. I knew it was best to let him go. I knew Sydney and most likely many other girls would go after him, try to get his attention. Because he was handsome and the quarterback on the football team.

But I knew he was much more than that. He was interesting and really smart and nice. I knew too much about Ox. And none of it would help me win mathletes competitions.

"I gotta go," I mumbled. I stuck my head deeper into my locker. I counted to ten and when I came out, Ox was gone. The hallways were full of people, but I felt very alone.

Just the way I'd planned it.

Nineteen

FINAL DRESS REHEARSAL
A Few Days Later—Friday

"I can't believe it's final dress rehearsal. I'm so nervous," I heard Tess say. "I think I'm going to throw up!"

Stage fright! That feeling of knowing you're going onstage in front of a crowd of people. You might feel shaky! Or sweaty and clammy! Or like you're going to throw up!

Emma had told me what to do for stage fright. She'd learned her methods from years of spelling bees, mathletes, and accepting awards for being the best student our elementary school ever had.

Take a deep breath. Breathe in through your nose, out through your mouth. Press one nostril closed and breathe through the other one. Then switch.

I closed my eyes and pretended I, too, had stage fright and thought I was going to throw up. But I didn't, because while everyone upstairs was freaking out for final dress rehearsal,

I was under the stage clearing out room to store all the stage props after the show. I could hear Tess and the cast directly above me through the ceiling door.

"This is our final run-through, people," Mrs. Burkle said. "The play is tomorrow! Focus, people, focus!"

I'd seen the set and everyone wearing their costumes on the way in. Everything did look pretty cool. The Yellow Brick Road, which I'd lined up myself brick by brick in the stage basement, looked especially awesome, I thought.

"Dude!" I heard Reilly say. "My straw is itching like a beast!"

Even covered in straw Reilly also had looked especially awesome. I'd seen him on the way in wearing the green Scarecrow hat, overalls, and triangle nose. Okay, maybe it wasn't his best look, but his piercing blue eyes still shone through.

Ah.

Then all of a sudden I heard a huge gasp. And people started going, "Awesome! Check it out! Cool!"

"Hurrah! Bravo!" Mrs. Burkle shouted. "Glinda's bubble has arrived!"

"My bubble?" Sydney squealed.

Glinda, of course, arrived in a see-through bubble when she first met Dorothy. I knew that Nick was psyched about what he'd found to use as a bubble. But they'd had to special order it and it hadn't arrived until today.

Everyone was still going, "That's so cool!" So I had to see

what it was. I climbed up the ladder and peeked my head out for a view.

Oh my gosh! Okay, that *was* cool. Nick was rolling something down the aisles. It was a plastic see-through circle that was bigger than he was. It looked like a giant clear hamster ball.

"Nick!" Mrs. Burkle clasped her hands with joy. "You've outdone yourself!"

"You climb in and walk around," Nick said. "Sydney, you need to get in it and practice walking."

I saw Sydney, wearing the beautiful pink Glinda dress, put her hands on her hips and frown.

"I have to get in *that*?" Sydney asked. "I thought I'd float down from the ceiling in a light bubble, that would pop as I made my entrance. Like in the movie."

"Are you kidding?" Nick asked. "What do you think this is—a major motion picture? I can't pull that off!"

"This is fabulous!" Mrs. Burkle announced. "Now, climb in."

"That thing is sweet, dude!" Reilly said. "I'd rock that thing."

"Then Reilly, can you show me how to use it?" Sydney asked sweetly.

Reilly climbed in the giant ball. He did look like he was in a bubble!

"Okay, now just walk really slowly," Nick told him.

Reilly walked slowly, grinning. When the bubble hit one of the audience chairs, it bounced off a little. Everyone laughed. Reilly went a little faster and bounced off a wall like a pinball. Then the giant ball was bouncing off walls left and right.

Sydney was seriously lucky. Not only did it look fun, but the audience was going to love the special effect! I stuck my head out the trapdoor even farther to watch as Reilly rolled himself in the bubble down the aisle and bumped off the stage.

Just then Sydney's pink slipper appeared right next to my nose. One more step and she was going to stomp right on me. I quickly closed the trapdoor a little bit so she wouldn't notice me.

"Tess, you look so cute in your Dorothy dress!" I heard Sydney say. "You're like the best actress ever! I hope I'm half as good as you."

Ugh, now I really was going to throw up.

"That's so nice of you," Tess answered. "But you're a great actress, too! You make a perfect Glinda. And you look gorgeous in that dress."

Gak.

"Aw, thanks," Sydney said. "You always look gorgeous. I mean, like your hair? It's uhmazing! Hey! I'm going to the mall this weekend with Cashmere. You should totally come with us!"

I suddenly had a flashback. The first time I met Sydney in homeroom she complimented my skirt. She invited me to the mall. She totally sucked me in with her PopularPersonality!

Then she squashed me flat as a bug when she humiliated me and dropped me publicly when I stood up to her. (And oozed a burrito all over the lunch table.) Sydney was using her EvilPopularCharm to suck Tess in!

Tess was the new Payton!

Tess! I silently begged. *Say no! Don't do it!*

"Um, okay," Tess said.

Noooo! Tess was sucked in! And then I realized what that meant for me. There was no way Sydney was going to share her with me. Bye, Tess. You were a good friend while it lasted.

Sigh.

Could I be any more left out? No! No, I could not. I needed a break from this. They could bond and become BFFs. They could dress rehearsal their play. They could float off together looking gorgeous in their plastic bubble. But that didn't mean I had to be tortured by any of it. I stumbled out of the stage basement, blinking back tears.

I stood in the hall and leaned against a locker. I just needed to breathe air that wasn't under the stage.

"Hi, Payton," someone said. It was Ox.

Ox! Ox who broke my sister's heart and stomped on it into a million teeny pieces! He was walking down the hallway to me.

I narrowed my eyes and glared at him. There. Now he'd go away.

"So," Ox said. "What's up?"

Or, he would stop and lean against the locker next to me.

I glared at him again. What's up? Well, for starters, you dumped my sister! My sister, who didn't even want to like a boy until you came along and used your EvilPopularCharm to suck her into your trap!! You squashed her flat as a bug and dropped her publicly!

And look what happened! Emma was so crushed she turned back into the old Emma! The Emma where people don't matter and she didn't care about anything but her school-work!

She wouldn't even hang out with anyone . . . including me.

I scowled at Ox fiercely and started walking.

"You two twins are masters of freezing me out," Ox said. "But just do me one favor. Just tell me what I did wrong."

"You hurt my sister," I replied. "Maybe she's awkward with boys and things and maybe she seems like a totally cold-fish person when she's doing her mathletes and stuff. But you really hurt her."

"I hurt her?" Ox looked confused.

I turned to him. "I know you didn't want to be boyfriend/girlfriend or whatever," I said. "But Emma really liked you, ok? And then you have to go and dump her. And now she's ignoring everyone—even me—and it's all your fault!"

There. I'd said it. Emma might not be happy about it, but I couldn't let this boy just squish her heart like a little bug.

"Payton," Ox said slowly. "I didn't dump Emma. *She* dumped *me*."

Wait. What?

"She dumped you?" I asked him.

"I thought things were cool," Ox said, looking miserable. "I know Emma is too busy for a boyfriend, but we were hanging out and then one day she said she was too busy to even talk to me. Even *talk* to me. Bam. That was it. Over."

My jaw dropped open.

"So you didn't crush her heart, causing her to become the old Stressed-Out-Only-My-Grades-Matter Emma?" I asked him.

Ox shook his head.

"I thought it was you," I said. "So wait. Then what *did* cause it?"

"I don't know," Ox said. "But if there is a way to change it back, let me know."

Wow. Ox looked really sad.

"I miss Emma," Ox said sadly.

Aw. He really liked my sister.

Something needed to be done about this. Because, I missed Emma, too.

What could have made Emma change back, if it wasn't Ox?

"Something doesn't add up here," I said.

"Add up!" Ox suddenly got a look of panic on his face. "Adding! Subtracting! Exponential carrying! I have to get back to mathletes! I was just taking a bathroom break!"

And Ox raced off down the hall, muttering math things.

Okay, he *was* perfect for my sister. So Tess might be perfect for Sydney. I might be perfect for nobody at all.

But Ox + Emma = Perfect Match. How to get Emma to realize that? That was one math equation I was going to figure out.

Twenty

SATURDAY MORNING MATHLETES COMPETITION

"Ladies and gentleman, we are down to the final three mathletes," the announcer's voice boomed from her clip-on microphone out into the audience.

Three hours and seventeen minutes ago, our first mathletes competition had begun. One written exam and one Top 20 head-to-head competition later, it was down to the final three.

Destiny Robinson from Vyse Avenue Prep School, Rajeev Sundeep from Shaker Heights, our rival public middle school,

and...

Emma Mills from—well, you know—it's ME!!!

I was sitting onstage, grinning. Because, well, I had just watched Jazmine "Fourth Place" James mess up a question and take a seat in the audience.

Buh-bye.

Okay, Jazmine seemed to have a cold, as evidenced by her bright-red nose, ever-present tissue box (which the judges checked to make sure had no hints or cheats on it), and at least two sneezing fits.

Her last answer sounded like "elebed" instead of "eleven," due to her stuffed-up nose. Of course, both "elebed" and "eleven" were incorrect. So sorry. Sit down in the seat of shame between your parents.

Hee.

I looked out into the audience at my parents. My mom smiled. My dad looked nervous. Payton, sitting next to them, gave me a thumbs-up. It made me feel good to have my own little rooting section in the filled-to-capacity auditorium of Shaker Heights Middle School. They had a nicer auditorium than we did, I'd noticed, but at least there were NO GECKOS. Their school mascot looked to be some kind of elf. Maybe a leprechaun . . .

"Emma Mills. Your problem is . . ." The announcer read it from her note cards.

I stood up, walked over to the standing uniform, and performed some mental calculations.

"One thousand and seventy-one square meters," I said.

"Correct!" the three judges said simultaneously.

"Go, Emma!" a familiar voice called out, amongst all the applause.

It was number seven, Ox. Ox had made the Top 10 and

then beat three really tough competitors. Secretly, I had been so happy and proud for him. Outwardly, I showed no emotion. This was my game face, and game on!

Two rounds passed, then Destiny went down on a proportional reasoning problem.

I looked at Rajeev.

He looked at me.

In that moment, it was just the two of us and math. The rest of the world—Jazmine, Payton, and even Ox—faded out of my mind.

Rajeev's turn . . . Correct!

Emma's turn . . . Correct!

Rajeev's turn . . . Correct!

Emma's turn. Uh-oh, this was a bad one. I wasn't sure about my answer . . . Correct!

Rajeev's turn.

"I'm sorry," the head judge said. "That is incorrect. Emma Mills must answer this next problem to become today's winner."

It was an algebraic expressions problem. Have I mentioned how much I l-o-v-e algebra? Especially when I give the correct answer and win the first mathletes competition!

"You won!" Payton cried, and rushed to the stage to give me a hug.

Then I had to get my picture taken holding my trophy. Then a picture between Rajeev and Destiny.

Finally, I was set free to celebrate. My parents, Coach Babbitt, and Counselor Case were all in a group. When I reached them they were all "Congratulations!" . . . "You were wonder-ful, honey!" and "You should be so proud of yourself!"

And I was. Proud of myself. Proud, excited, a little dizzy, and . . . something else. An emotion I couldn't identify.

"See you at Swirly's!" I heard someone say. Swirly's was a nearby ice-cream and sorbet shoppe.

My family was not going to Swirly's. Because it was not just a big day for me, it was the night of Payton's play.

"It's not my play," Payton grumbled whenever my parents called it that. "I'm not even *in* it. Just under it."

"I'm sure your behind-the-scenes efforts have helped," my mother told Payton. "Any activity you've contributed to, we want to support."

"Yes! We are *so* there!" my father said.

"Dad!" I hissed.

"Shhh . . . ," Payton shushed.

I held my six-inch trophy in one hand and dragged my dad toward the exit with the other.

Just before we reached it, I heard someone say, "Congratu-lations, Emma."

I turned. It was Ox.

"I know how much this means to you," Ox said. He had his hands in his jeans pockets and looked a little . . . sad.

"Thanks," I said. I wanted to say something meaningful back. But keeping away from Ox had been the right thing to do. No matter how wrong it felt. Because, I was the mathletes champion! Emma = Winner. My goals had to be clear.

"Are you going to Swirly's?" Ox asked me.

"No." I shook my head. "We're going to the school play."

"Well," Ox said, "see ya." And he walked out the exit door.

And then *they* walked by.

"Claudine! Martin!" my father called out.

Mr. and Mrs. James stopped next to my family. With, of course, Jazmine.

"Great first competition, huh?" my dad said cluelessly. "Our girls really know their stuff!"

The Jameses all just looked at my trophy.

"Jaz!" Hector called. "Swirly's?"

"No!" Mr. and Mrs. James said simultaneously.

"Jazmine has a bad head cold," Mr. James said. "She needs to go right home to bed."

As my family (well, my parents) waved them good-bye, we heard Jazmine's mother.

"Right to bed with your math books," Mrs. James said to Jazmine. "The next competition is in just ten weeks, and you, young lady, *you* will be holding that trophy."

Jazmine sneezed. The only thing she was holding now was a tissue to her nose. I almost felt sorry for her, with a pushy mom like that. Suddenly, a white something came flying through the air and landed in my trophy.

Payton and I looked in.

"Ewww. It's a tissue." I grimaced.

"A *used* tissue." Payton gagged.

"Jazmine boogers," we both groaned. "Gross!"

I wanted to tell Jazmine to take it out, but she and her parents were long gone.

So here I was, holding a trophy full of Jazmine sneeze. As the last of the mathletes and their families left the building, laughing and joking around, I did not feel quite as happy as I'd expected.

I mean, I'd gotten what I'd wanted. (Hadn't I?) Yes! I had won.

Twenty-one

SATURDAY EVENING
Backstage Before the Play

"Toto!" Tess cried out dramatically as an eighth-grade girl was tying a bow into the end of each of her braids. "Where's Toto?"

"You sound very convincing," I said to Tess. "But I think the line is 'Toto, come back!' when Toto runs after the Wicked Witch."

"No, I really mean, where is Toto?" Tess wailed. "My stuffed Toto is missing! I can't find him! I can't be Dorothy without my Toto!"

"Um, Tess?" I said. I pointed to the chair, where her blue-and-white checked dress was puffed out. "You're sitting on him."

"Oh," Tess said, pulling the stuffed terrier out from under her petticoat. "Thanks. Wait! Where's my bow?"

"In your hair." The eighth grader sighed.

Tess was really nervous. But I didn't blame her. The play was tonight! I'd come to the school with my family after Emma's big mathletes win. Emma and my parents were out getting their tickets, and taking their seats with the rest of the audience.

Mrs. Burkle had asked me to help out backstage. When she'd asked, I'd thought she was going to say *under* the stage, so this was a relief. I watched everyone getting the final touches to their stage makeup and costumes. I saw Nick checking the light boards. I saw Mrs. Burkle running around like a crazy person.

And I saw Tess practically hyperventilating.

"Take deep breaths," I told Tess. "In the nose, out through the mouth."

Tess breathed in and out. I hoped that was helpful.

"Payton!" Mrs. Burkle raced over to me. "What are you doing?"

"Um, helping Tess breathe," I said.

"Breathe? I would think she could breathe on her own, yes?" Mrs. Burkle said loudly. "Come with me!"

I didn't have time to explain the whole breathing thing, so I just followed Burkle across the stage. She stopped to talk to The Munchkins and signaled for me to wait a minute.

And that's when I saw more munchkins backstage. Named Mason and Jason. And Emma was chasing them.

"Payton! Save me! Your sister is after me!" One of them ducked behind me.

"What are you guys doing back here?" I asked. I turned to Emma. "Are they allowed backstage?"

"No!" Emma said. "That's why I'm after them! First, they came and sat with me in the audience. They begged! They pleaded! I couldn't say no to their mother, the woman who holds my future in her hands, could I? But instead of staying with me, the boys took off!"

Oh.

"Boys!" Emma tried again. "We *have* to get back to our seats."

"No way, I have to find Nick," Mason said. "I want to see if he can use my fart noise in the show!"

"He meant *after* the play, perhaps next week," Emma said. "Not *tonight!*"

And that's when I saw it. Peeking out of Mason's sleeve was the gecko. I looked over at Emma. She didn't notice it. I had to get her out of there.

"Mason." I leaned over to him. "You've got to put the gecko—"

"Dude!" Mason interrupted. "What is *that?* That is COOL!"

Mason was pointing to the giant Glinda-bubble. And then he was running over to it!

"Mason!" Emma yelled to him, chasing after him. "Do not touch that!"

Then we all ran after Mason, who suddenly stopped when he got to the ball and looked daze. He was gazing up at someone.

"You're pretty," he said.

Ugh. It was Sydney.

"Yes," she said. "I know."

"Come on," Emma urged him. "We have to get out of here."

"Oh, ew," Sydney said. "It's the Wonder Twins. As in, I wonder why the twins are backstage?"

"I'm not backstage," Emma said, gritting her teeth. "Boys, we have to leave."

"Yup, let's go somewhere else," I agreed. "Sydney, good luck!"

"You're supposed to say, 'Break a leg,'" she said. "But since you're not an actor, I guess you wouldn't know that. Saying 'Good luck' actually means bad luck."

"Actually, that's why I said it," I retorted.

I'd actually wanted to tell her to break a leg . . . and an arm . . . and her nose. But I stopped myself. I should not stoop to Sydney's level. Or, actually, rise to her level. Hmm. Sydney was looking seriously tall. Much, much higher up than usual. She was wearing a leotard thing, tights, and really high sparkly heels.

Mrs. Burkle suddenly appeared. "Sydney! Why aren't you dressed? Payton, help Sydney get dressed."

Sydney and I both looked at each other, and found a moment of solidarity.

"It's okay!" Sydney and I both said at the same time.

"I don't need help," Sydney said.

"Obviously you do, since you're not wearing your gown. Payton. Help. Sydney. Get. Dressed," Mrs. Burkle commanded again.

Ugh.

"Fine. Hold my gown for a second, while I fix the strap on my shoe," Sydney said. "Aren't my shoes to die for? You recognize the label, right? Or, wait, was that your sister who was fashionable. I always get you two confused."

Grrr. I took Sydney's gown and didn't say a word.

"Hey, Sydney." Nick came over. "You need to take a practice run in your bubble. Don't forget to take off those shoes."

"I'm not taking off my shoes," Sydney said. "I just put these on! Hello, designer shoes? In pink sparkly? They match my Glinda gown perfectly."

"They're heels," Nick said, patiently.

"I know, but ew, the costume had ugly slipper things." Sydney waved him off. "I'm not wearing those. I mean, look at the sparkles on these shoes! Aren't they amazing?!"

"Sure," Nick said. "But not for the bubble. You won't be able to walk in those things in the bubble."

"Yes, I will," Sydney said. "I'm an expert in heels."

Sydney went over to the bubble and jumped in.

"Wait!" Nick called to her.

But Sydney started walking around in the ball.

"Cool! She's like a giant hamster," Mason marveled. "A giant, beautiful hamster princess."

"I estimate that ball's circumference is at least one hundred times the size of her head," Jason marveled.

And Sydney has a very big head, I thought. With her ego.

"She *can* walk in heels," I admitted. That was impressive. The few times I'd tried to walk in heels, I'd wobbled and tipped over. But Sydney was walking fine, even in a giant plastic ball.

"Oops!" Sydney said as the ball bounced off one of the Munchkins.

"Excuse me!" Sydney called out. But, wait, the ball was rolling backward. And then—*bounce!* It bounced off one of the trees.

"Sydney!" Nick waved frantically. "Sit down! Don't walk!"

"I got it!" Sydney scoffed. She walked again and the ball rolled. Sydney tipped a little.

"Does she have control of that thing?" Emma asked as Sydney wobbled around backstage. "I think her equalizing angles are off."

"No duh," Jason agreed. "She needs to maintain acute angles of motion or she's going to roll off the stage."

"Oh, no! The Hamster Princess needs saving!" Mason said. "I'll rescue her! I'll be her superhero!" Mason ran over and threw his arms around the ball and stopped it.

"I'm fine, you rugrat!" Sydney said, all snotty.

Mason looked a little hurt. I felt sorry for him for a moment.

"Let go of my bubble!" Sydney said to him, and kicked at the ball where Mason was, just as he let go. And then it started rolling again. Sydney suddenly looked freaked. The ball started veering toward the curtain at the front of the stage! Oh, no! She was going to roll through the curtain and off the stage!

She tried to regain her balance and then—*boom!* She fell over!

"Oh, good," Jason said. "She sat down, so her center of gravity stopped the ball!"

Except Sydney didn't look very happy. She was clutching her shoe.

"My ankle!" she wailed. "I hurt my ankle!"

We all rushed over to her.

"Oh, my!" Mrs. Burkle said. "Is there an injury? We must get that checked by a medical professional! Sydney's understudy must take her place!"

Sydney stopped wailing.

"I'm okay!" she said. "I can go on!"

She stood up. And then fell over.

"Sydney's ankle is swollen," Jason said, leaning over to inspect it. "Could be a sprain or strain."

"Somebody fetch Sydney's parents," Mrs. Burkle said. "They must take her to the hospital to get it checked."

"No! I can still do it!" Sydney said.

But when she stood up, she couldn't put any weight on her foot.

"Sorry, school policy," Burkle said. Nick raced out as Cashmere rushed in.

"Oh, no," Cashmere said. "I heard you screaming and came to see what happened. Now you can't play Glinda! And don't you have a big game to cheer at tomorrow?"

"I'll let the coach know you have to miss that, too," Burkle said.

"Agh! Shush, Cashmere!" Sydney wailed some more.

"Who's the understudy for Glinda?" Mrs. Burkle asked. "Oh, goodness, it's Zahra."

Zahra was already covering for the Mayor of the Lollipop Kids, who had gotten the flu.

"We have no Glinda!" Mrs. Burkle cried. "Oh, goodness!"

"Payton knows the lines!" Emma volunteered.

"Shhh." I hissed and elbowed her.

"Is this true?" Burkle peered at me. "Do you know the lines?"

Um. Yeah. I did. I nodded.

"Then, quickly! Put on Glinda's dress! I will let the cast know!" Burkle said. "Payton is the New Sydney!"

"What?" Sydney shrieked. "Payton is not the New Sydney! Payton is the New Poopy!"

"Payton is in!" Burkle announced emphatically. "Sydney is out!"

"I can do it! I can—" I heard Sydney wailing as her parents carried her away.

Oh my gosh. Ohmygoshohmygosh.

"Payton," Mrs. Burkle said. "This will look good on your school service record. Payton steps up as needed! But, oh, dear, why is our Tin Man's body on backward? I am needed else-where!"

"What are you thinking?" I hissed at Emma. "I'm not pre-pared! I can't do this!"

"You *can* do it," Emma said firmly.

This was too overwhelming. I couldn't just go up there onstage with practically no warning and totally no practice!

"Just put on the dress," Emma said, holding out the pink Glinda dress to me.

"I can't," I said, backing away. "I'm not prepared! I'm pan-icking!"

"It's just stage fright," Emma said. "Breathe deeply. Don't panic."

Then suddenly the Glinda-ball rolled past us. Mason and Jason were playing soccer with the Glinda-ball.

"Boys!" Emma called out. "Don't mess with that ball!"

And then Emma gasped. And pointed. The gecko was peeking out of Mason's sleeve.

"Emma!" I said. "Breathe deeply! Don't panic!"

"Geckophobia," Emma croaked. She stood there frozen, her eyes wide. She was panicking. And then the gecko took a flying leap.

"Oh, no!" Mason cried. "Mascot!"

The gecko leaped onto the rubber Glinda-bubble and bounced off! It landed on the floor! And ran and then . . . dis-appeared.

"Where did he go?" Mason cried louder. "Mascot!"

"Under the stage," Jason said, leaning over. "There appears to be a crack leading under the stage."

The stage basement room!

"Save him!" Mason was now hysterically crying.

I looked at Mason. I knew what I had to do.

"I'm going in," I announced. Emma stood frozen, in fear of the gecko on the loose. "I know the stage basement. I'll go down really fast and be back before you know it."

I hung the Glinda dress on Emma's shoulder.

"I'll be right back," I said.

"Go, Gecko," Emma said weakly.

Emma

Twenty-two

STILL BACKSTAGE BEFORE THE PLAY

I was holding a sparkling pink pouf of a dress while trying to calm the terror twins.

"Jason, Mason," I said quietly but firmly. "Don't call any attention to us. Just wait patiently and Payton will be right back."

"Wait Payton-ly?" Jason joked.

"Shut up, Jay," Mason said. His voice sounded strange. Was he about to cry? "Mascot never runs away! What if she can't find him? What if he hides for two years like that gecko in the library?"

"It'll be okay, Mason," I said. Sheesh, my hand was getting tired. This dress was heavy. "Payton will get him. She's braver than I am."

"I have an irrational fear of small reptiles. She doesn't."

"Mason has an irrational fear of the dark," Jason said.

"Oh, yeah?" Mason frowned. "You're afraid of bugs! And thunderstorms. And . . . girls!"

"Boys!" I broke in. I had to shut them up. "Um . . . I am the Good Witch Glinda and I-er-banish all fears from you."

I spotted Glinda's/Sydney's star-shaped wand on a table. I grabbed it. Then I tapped the twins lightly on their heads. They both giggled. I was getting pretty good at this kid thing.

"Payton!" Mrs. Burkle's voice boomed.

Oh, good. Payton is back!

I looked around. Where was my twin? I didn't see her.

"Payton!" Mrs. Burkle said again. Closer. To me.

I froze.

"Payton, why aren't you dressed?" Mrs. Burkle shrieked. "We need you ready right now!"

Uh. I couldn't figure out how to explain that my sister was under the stage rescuing a gecko that Mason should not have brought in the first place. Mason would get in trouble or Payton would or the play wouldn't start or . . .

"Okay," I choked out. I took the dress off the hanger and gave the boys a look that said, *Keep your mouths shut, please?* I put the glittery pouf over my head and slipped the dress on over my clothes. Whew. It fit over my new MATHLETES ROCK! tee, my jeans, and just barely hit the ground covering my sneakers.

Oh, yeah. This hemline was so much better than with Sydney's high heels. And the style was more suited to flats. Those heels took away from the gown. Less can be more.

"Payton!" Mrs. Burkle said. "Don't forget your wand!"

❀ 187 ❀

"Thank you," I said and grabbed the sparkly star-shaped wand. "You can go back to the other people now." I waved the wand in the direction of the real backstage, where all the action was going on before the curtain went up.

I was only wearing this costume temporarily, because Payton was going to be back any second. And when she got here, Mrs. Burkle couldn't still be here.

I had to text my sister to hurry up. I reached into my jeans pocket—Oh! The dress! I fumbled around and—yes—I found an opening near my side where the skirt wrapped around in layers. I could feel my jeans! I could feel my cell phone.

Why was Mrs. Burkle still standing here?

"Payton, we don't have time to dally," my English teacher/Payton's drama coach said. "Come with me NOW."

"Boys, wait here," I hissed. "I'll be right back."

As I reluctantly followed Mrs. Burkle, I heard Jason say, "I knew it! She's pretending to be Payton again! They're switching places like they did in the library."

Great. Can't fool a genius twin. I should know. I'd have to swear them to secrecy later for the greater good of all of us. . . .

Wait a minute! Two boys were rolling the gigantic bubble over to me.

"Glinda," Mrs. Burkle said. "Get in."

Get in the bubble? No way. This was going too far.

"Glinda," Mrs. Burkle said, her voice tight. "I have to

supervise you for safety purposes before I can get back to the other actors. Now, please get in."

I climbed in. Whoa. Weird. I waved to Mrs. Burkle, who, thankfully, ran backstage. I was stuck in a midway point—an area that was away from the actors and scenery. I knew this, because I could hear muffled, panicky voices—Tess? That Reilly guy Payton had a crush on?—but I couldn't see anyone.

Boy this bubble was foggy. And warm. Where the heck was Payton??? I reached again for my cell, pulled it out, and texted my twin.

Come up!!! 911!!

And waited.

After an eternity—okay two minutes and three seconds—Payton texted back.

I'm trying!

She's trying? No! No trying! I replied:

Do it!

And waited. The world outside the bubble was eerily quiet. Except for applause, and then . . .

Whrrshhhhh!

A loud, windy sound came from the stage.

Oh. No. That couldn't be the tornado! (Could it?) The whirring noise stopped.

"'Toto?'" said Tess' voice, loud and clear. "'I don't think we're in Kansas anymore.'"

The play had started! I was supposed to be sitting in the audience; not encased in a bubble wearing a Good Witch costume. Could things get any worse?

Of course they could. Because two boys began rolling the bubble, and through the plastic I could see the stage. With Tess holding a stuffed dog. And a house with two feet sticking out from under it.

As the ball rolled, I felt myself tipping. Must locate my center of gravity. I experimented a bit with laws of balance and managed to keep on my feet. However, my forward velocity must have been greater than the boys' pushing force because I rolled right out of their hands. Onto the stage. Straight for Tess/Dorothy! At the last moment, I lurched crazily to the left and missed running over the lead actress. Instead, I crashed into the house.

I heard some gasps from the audience.

Audience??? Have I mentioned I have severe stage fright? Only in competitions, armed with extensive knowledge, can I stand up in front of other people.

In a bubble in a dress in a play I'm not supposed to be in? Nope. The crash against the house spun me around and knocked me over. I sat, stunned, in a pouf of confusion.

Tess/Dorothy stared at me. The audience stared at me. Payton would be telling me to stand up and pretend to be her. So, I summoned my inner Payton, stood up in the bubble, and waved my star wand and smiled.

Some cheers from the audience.

Okay. Now what? The whole auditorium was silent.

And then—"Twinkle, twinkle, little star"—my cell phone ringtone went off. The audience started to laugh.

I ruffled through poufiness and found the opening in the dress. I took out my phone.

"Hello?" I said, chirping in a high-pitched voice that I hoped sounded Glinda-like.

"Emma, I'm trapped under the stage," Payton's voice said into my ear. "I can hear you. Just do what I say."

"Yes, this is Glinda," I said, my voice shaky with terror. I felt a thumping under my feet. Payton??

The audience was really laughing now.

"Say, 'Are you a good witch or a bad witch?'" Payton said.

What? Was that like one of those Top 10 Dumb Twin Questions people ask—like which one is the good twin and which one is the evil twin?

"Just say the line!" Payton hissed. And thumped harder. My bubble wobbled.

Oh! The line!

"'Are you a GOOD witch or a BAD witch?'" I asked Dorothy. "Um . . . my friend wants to know." I pointed to the phone with my wand.

"'Why, I'm not a witch at all,'" Tess/Dorothy said, staring at me like I was crazy.

Suddenly, a bunch of students covered with face makeup came out onto the stage, walking on their knees.

"Oh!" I said. "The Munchkins!"

"Yes," said one knee-walker. "'I am a Munchkin of Munchkin-land.'"

And, thank goodness, The Munchkins started talking with Dorothy.

"What do I do?" I whispered into the phone.

"You have one more line, then get the heck off the stage," Payton said. *Thump, thump.*

I tried not to look out into the audience, because of my stage fright, but my bubble ball turned that way a bit. Through the plastic and with all the stage lights, I couldn't really see anybody. Just a blur. I felt better. Like I could do this. Maybe.

Just one more line. What was it? I clutched my phone. Oops. Hit the off button. Klutz.

I felt banging under my sneakers. It made the bubble vibrate. Vibrate! My cell was going *brzzzt.* A text from Payton.

Ur line is, "Follow the Yellow Brick Road!"

I watched until Dorothy and The Munchkins stopped talking. They looked at me. I took a deep breath.

"'Follow the Yellow Brick' . . . whoa!" The bubble started wobbling. I barely kept my balance as I realized the stage was rising! Earthquake? No, no, just a trapdoor. I looked down through the plastic bottom and saw . . .

Payton's face! Through a little opening in the stage, Payton peered up at me. She looked as surprised as I felt. I looked at Tess/Dorothy and thought fast. I stepped to the side so my big poufy skirt covered up the hole in the floor and my twin in the hole.

"'Follow the Yellow Brick Road!'" I shouted, a little more Loud Witch than Good Witch.

And then I felt it. A crawling sensation around my socks. I flashed back to the crawling feeling of the mascot gecko in my hair.

Eeeee.

"Don't be silly, Emma," I told myself in my head. *"It's just that being onstage has freaked you out."* I felt and heard the trap-door shutting under me. Okay. Payton was gone. I could leave my spot.

"'Good-bye, Dorothy!'" I waved as I pushed my way back in the direction from which I'd made my stage debut. "'Follow the Yellow Brick Road!'"

And I was out of the spotlight and off the stage.

Twenty-three

DURING PLAY, UNDER STAGE

I was sitting in total darkness. Pitch-black, under the stage, in the stage basement . . . with a gecko on the loose!

This was *so* not what I'd imagined. But it figured. When I'd come downstairs, the main door locked behind me. And to make it ten thousand times worse, the lights wouldn't go on. Nick had turned them off when he ran the light board upstairs. I only had the little light from my cell phone. Which was losing battery strength, so it was barely glowing. I'd ended up feeling around in the darkness for the lizard. I could hear his little tiny feet scampering around. At least I knew my way around the room, since I'd been here so often. But I had no luck catching the gecko.

My brilliant idea of letting in some light by opening the trapdoor? Fail. I'd popped up under the stage and totally freaked out Emma in the Glinda ball.

At least Emma had her phone with her, so we could get her through the play. Kind of, anyway.

I heard her voice upstairs: "'Follow the Yellow Brick Road!'"

After u follow Yellow Brick Rd, follow curtain 2 the door in floor. Unlock & get me out!

I finished texting Emma and waited. I could hear applause. I could hear laughter. I could hear my crazy sister rolling off the stage.

I sat down on the paint can and waited. And waited. *Hello?*

Emma! Rescue me!

No answer. Argh. I tried to push the trapdoor open to see what was going on. But it was stuck! Something was on top of the trapdoor!

I went to text Emma again and—oh, no! My cell phone battery died! I had no light! No phone! No way of reaching the outside world! Was I going to be stuck down here forever?!!!

Then I realized that other than the door onstage I had texted her about, Emma might not know how else to get into the stage basement. She didn't know about the main door. I felt my way over to the other door in the ceiling. I carefully climbed up on the ladder and knocked on the ceiling. I hoped someone was up there. *Knock! Knock!*

And then the trapdoor opened up! YES! I was rescued!

"Payton!" said one of the Mason/Jason twins, sticking his head in. "Did you find Mascot?"

"I did but I lost him," I said. "He jumped again. I'm so sorry."

"Oh, no!" he said. And he closed the door.

Wait! Closed the door? Noooo! I thumped on the ceiling again. Let me out!!! The door opened up again.

"Mason, you have to let me out!" I said to him.

"Payton, shut the door or Mascot might escape!" Mason said. He started to close the door again.

"Mason, *I* need to escape," I said. "Let me out of here!"

"But you didn't find Mascot." His little sad face looked back at me. "Are you just going to give up?"

Oh, great. I felt terrible.

"I promise I'll find him," I said. But I had to get out of that basement. "I just need to go get supplies. Um, flashlights and things."

Mason sighed, and let me climb out of the basement.

"First, where's Emma?" I asked him.

"Emma's hiding in one of the dressing areas," Mason said, and led me over to where she was. "She doesn't want to get busted being you. It's so cool how you guys traded places. Does Emma take your math tests for you?"

"No!" I said. "We don't do anything like that. And you and Jason shouldn't, either."

"Bummer," Mason said.

"Did you find him?" Jason asked.

"No," I said. "But I will. First I need to talk to Emma."

I hurried to find Emma, with the boys right behind me.

"Payton! Quick!" Emma said. "Change clothes with me! Here, put on Glinda's dress! We don't have much time. They're doing a Scarecrow scene, so if you hurry you'll be ready for the next one!"

"I can't," I said. "I have to find Mascot first. I couldn't get him."

"Payton, you tried," Emma said. "You did your best. Now just switch back with me. This is your chance! You've wanted to be onstage! Come on!"

"I promised the boys," I said.

"Oh," Emma said. Then she sighed. "I'll help the boys find Mascot."

"You will?" Mason, Jason, and I all said, shocked.

"Yes," Emma said. "If he's that important to you, I will find him. I have overcome my fear of being onstage. I will now overcome my fear of creepy little green lizards."

She closed her eyes and took a deep breath.

"I'm ready. Although if we see him, you guys will grab him. Avoid contact with me at all costs," she added. "But first, wait for me out there while Payton and I switch clothes."

"Wow," I said. "Impressive."

"Shhhh," Emma said. "Quick and switch before anyone realizes that it was me out there."

Emma pulled the pink Glinda dress over her head. Underneath, she had on her mathletes competition shirt that said MATHLETES CHAMP.

And on the front of her shirt . . . was the gecko. Stuck right to the CHAMP.

"Um," I said.

"Hurry!" Emma said. "If we switch really fast, Burkle will never know!"

"Um," I said, and tried to reach out subtly to pluck the gecko off her.

"What are you—" Emma looked down and froze. "Oh. Hello. There is a creepy little green lizard on my well-earned mathletes championship T-shirt."

"Breathe deep," I said. "In through one nostril. Out through the other. Don't panic."

I leaned out and waved Mason to come over.

"Mascot!" he said, his eyes lighting up. But then Mascot crawled into Emma's hair. Oh, no. I waited for her to freak out.

"Emma." Mason's eyes lit up. "Mascot really likes you. I think it's your supershiny hair."

"Really?" Emma asked, still frozen. "My supershiny hair?"

"Yeah," Mason said. "Your hair is so shiny."

"Wait a minute," I said. "I have supershiny hair, too. In fact, I'm the twin who is taller, with the bigger nose, and *with the shinier hair*."

"I don't know." Emma suddenly smiled. "The gecko is only attracted to my hair. Not yours. Hmm. I think that's proof."

"Hey," I said. I reached out and plucked the gecko off her hair. Then I put him on mine. "See, he likes mine, too."

And then the gecko jumped back to Emma's head. And she didn't even flinch.

"My hair is shinier!" I whined.

"It's okay," Mason said in a comforting voice. "Your nose is still bigger."

"Plus, Emma's hair smells really good," Jason said as he suddenly appeared behind me. "I noticed that when she tutors us. It smells like oranges and flowers."

"Well, Payton, it appears the gecko has solved that shiny-hair competition of ours." Emma looked quite pleased. And suddenly she plucked the gecko out of her hair. And cheerfully held it in her hand.

"But, Payton, your breath smells a lot better than Emma's," Mason added.

HAH!

"Okay," Emma said loudly. "Focus! We found the gecko. Mason, take Mascot and don't let him go. It's time for Payton to turn into Glinda."

Emma's calm was contagious. I slipped the dress over my head. My sneakers were hidden, so I kept them on.

"I should brush my hair," I said. "Since maybe that's why it's not as shiny as usual."

"Payton, get over the shiny-hair competition." Emma grinned. "And go break a leg. But not like Sydney."

"Well, at least let me get some stage makeup on," I said.

I went over to the dressing table and Glinda'd myself up. All those hours spent under the stage, behind the scenes, and I was finally going to be *on* the stage. In the spotlight.

I took a deep breath and headed out of the dressing area. And ran into Nick.

"Hey, Payton, I'm sorry the bubble is kind of out of control," Nick said. "I thought it was the coolest prop."

He looked disappointed. I thought about the hours he'd spent backstage, too.

"It *is* the coolest prop," I said. "It's not your fault Sydney wore those stupid heels and Emma is a klutz."

Oops. Nick looked at me oddly.

"*Emma* is a klutz?" Nick asked.

"Um," I said. "Nothing. Anyway, I am going to rock your bubble. Get that bubble ready. Here comes Glinda."

"Awesome!" he said. "And hey, you look really nice as Glinda."

"Scene 3!!!" Mrs. Burkle was yelling as she came through the area. "Glinda! Munchkins! Places, everyone! Be ready to go onstage."

I took a deep breath and got ready to go onstage.

Emma

Twenty-four

AFTER THE PLAY

"Woo-hoo!" I cheered.

"Yay, Payton!" Mason yelled. He was sitting in one of the auditorium chairs on my left.

"Yay, Tess and Nick!" I added loudly. Around us, the audience was clapping and cheering. The play was over. Dorothy had found her way home from Oz—with a little advice from my twin sister Glinda—and it was all a big success. The actors bowed and left the stage, and the auditorium lights went on overhead.

"The plot line was totally illogical," Jason said. He was seated on my right. "If there really was a tornado, why wasn't the Kansas set destroyed?"

"Jason, it's a *fantasy*," I told him. "It's not real life."

"Emma!" Speaking of real life—Counselor Case (responsible for my permanent record for college) and Coach Babbitt

❀ 201 ❀

(responsible for my mathletes career)—were making their way toward us.

"Emma, thank you for sitting with our boys," Counselor Case said. "It let us enjoy the play together. It was almost like our first date, when we went to see *our* high school's play. Remember, honey?"

"Ew!" . . . "Gross!" The twins gagged.

"Er, yes," my math coach said, looking a little uncomfortable. "Well, perhaps we should be leaving now."

Yes! After all the pressures of today—the mathletes competition (which I won!), babysitting, the gecko/bubble fiasco, and trying to impress everyone—I really needed a break.

"Payton asked me to stop by backstage after the play," I told Coach Babbitt. "So I'll be going in the opposite direction."

I began to walk down toward the stage, expecting the boys and their parents to walk upward toward the exit.

"Can we go backstage with Emma?" Mason begged. "I want to see Payton! Uh, I mean Nick! So I can, uh, see the sound effects!"

Spend more time with the Twins of Trouble? *Did I have to?* I started to shake my head no, but Jason stopped me.

"Mason," Jason said loudly, "who do you think was a better Glinda? Emma or Payton?"

"I'd be happy to take the boys, Coach," I said, grabbing one hand of each twin. "Can we meet you at the school entrance in fifteen minutes?"

"That's fine," Coach Babbitt said. "Anything for our math-letes champ!"

Then, as the grown-ups turned to leave, Counselor Case stopped.

"Oh, Emma!" she said. "Before I forget, this is for you." She handed me an envelope that had my name on it.

"And would you please give this one to your sister?" Counselor Case gave me another envelope. It said "Payton Mills."

"Of course." I smiled my perfect tutor/mathlete champion smile. And dragged Jason and Mason downward toward the stage.

"Umm . . . ," I said. "That part of the play where I was in the bubble? I was helping Payton out. So, it doesn't really count as switching places, right? Mason? Jason?"

"You were helping me and Mascot out," Mason said. "So Jason and I won't tell anybody."

"Ooh, a secret," Jason said. "Like the one about Mason being scared of brain-eating zombies?"

"Duh, who wouldn't be scared if a zombie came to eat your brain?" Mason sputtered.

"You of all people shouldn't be worried about that," Jason said, with a sly smile. "They'd go hungry. Get it? 'Cause you don't have a brain?"

"Well, if you tell anyone about the Payton-saving-Mascot-while-Emma-was-in-a-bubble *secret*, I'll tell *yours*," Mason shot back.

"You mean that I'm scared of bugs?" Jason's eyes grew wide.

"And thunderstorms. Big whoop. Your secrets are better. How about the secret that you think Payton is c-u-t-e. . . ."

Mason blushed and looked like he wanted to strangle his twin. I knew that look all too well. But, wait. Mason had a crush—on my sister? That was too awkward to even contemplate any further.

"Here we are!" I cut the twins off. "Backstage with all the famous stars! Hi, Dorothy/Tess! You were amazing!"

"Thanks, Emma!" Tess said. Her long blond hair had been taken out of the Dorothy pigtails and turned into crimpy waves.

"Payton's in a changing room," Tess told us. "She should be out soon. Wasn't she awesome taking over for Sydney like that? And she was so funny, too!" Tess laughed.

Yes. Funny. Ha.

"I didn't even know the bubble was zoned for cell phone use," a boy's voice said from behind me. It was Nick.

"Nick!" Jason said, jumping up and down. "Your special effects were spectacular. Mason said you have excellent technology. Did you know I'm quite proficient with technology? Can I watch you finish?"

"Sure, I've got a few more things to unplug." Nick smiled. "But first, everybody meet my family—Dad, my stepmom, Liz, my sister, Margaret. These are my friends Tess and . . ."

"Emma Mills!" Nick's younger sister said. "It's a pleasure to finally meet you in a noncompetitive arena."

"Margaret!" I smiled. "Spell 'corpuscle'!"

"Logorrhea!" Margaret said back.

"Spelling Bee talk," I explained to Mason and Jason. "Margaret was the youngest competitor at States last year."

"Wow!" Jason breathed, staring at Margaret.

"She's too old for you, doofus." Mason elbowed his brother.

"I'm almost nine," Jason retorted.

"I'll be ten in two weeks," Margaret said. "So I'll be eligible for spelling bee, Geobee, Scrabble-lympics, and—next year? Mathletes! Emma, when I get old like you, I want to be a champion just like you!"

"It *is* fun doing competitions," I agreed. "Even when you're old like me."

"It's all Margaret does," her father said. "Study, study, study."

And then it hit me. Margaret was like me. That was good in some ways. But what about the not-so-good parts?

"Margaret?" I said. "Is there anything else you're interested in? Besides academics?"

Margaret looked surprised. And a little shy.

"Um, well, I like beading. Making jewelry?"

"There's a beading class for kids at the craft store," Nick's stepmother said. "I keep offering to take her."

"It would interfere with my study schedule." Margaret frowned. "I can't afford to indulge in frivolous activities if I want to be a winner."

Oh, boy. Margaret was like a mini me.

❀ 205 ❀

"Emma understands," Margaret said. "Right, Emma?"

"I do understand," I said slowly. "It's fun and challenging to study and compete. And winning feels amazing. But winning isn't everything. And academics shouldn't be your only thing."

Just then, Payton came around the corner wearing her regular clothes. And with her was Quinn! I stood up straight and took a deep breath.

"I love math and competitions . . . and I also love fashion!" I announced loudly.

Margaret said, "Whoa."

"Ergh!" Jason made a strangling noise as Mason put him in a headlock. I ignored them and kept talking.

"In fact, one of the most fun things I want to do is a Passion-for-Fashion website with my friend Quinn."

Payton and Quinn had reached us. They both looked at me.

"Quinn painted the *Oz* set," I told everyone.

They all complimented Quinn.

"I'm hoping she'll hang out with me," I went on, "and teach me about art and other cool, creative things."

Please say you're still my friend, please be my friend, I said silently, looking at Quinn.

"But what about your studying and competitions?" Quinn asked. "Won't it get in your way?"

"Well, studying is a big part of my life," I said, looking back at Margaret. "But it shouldn't be my whole life. It's important to have balance. Creative outlets. Friends."

"Great!" Quinn said, smiling. "I'll text you and we'll set up a time. I've got some great new sites to show you, Emma! It'll be fun!"

"Cool!" I said, waving to Quinn as she left. "Fun!"

"Margaret," I said. "Spell 'zirconia.'"

"Z-i-r-c-o-n-i-a," Margaret said.

"See? Mathletes and fashion? Spelling bees and jewelry? That's what I mean. We can be fierce in competitions *and* in our hobbies."

Margaret laughed. Her dad and stepmom did, too.

Payton was weirdly quiet. Looking at me. Even though we couldn't read each other's minds (twin myth), I could make an educated guess as to what she was thinking.

"Who is this person? Not my twin sister, AcadEmma!"

"I feel all wobbly," Payton said. "Like I'm still in a bubble."

Okay. I can't even guess what's in her mind.

"Jason," Nick said. "Want to help me unplug the tech?"

"Yes!" Jason said as he followed Nick. Then he stopped and looked back. "Bye, Margaret!"

Margaret giggled and said good-bye to Jason, then the rest of us, as her parents said it was time to leave.

So it was down to Payton, Mason, and me. I was about to tell my sister how amazing a Glinda she'd been, when Mason beat me to it.

"You were amazing, Payton!" Mason said. Suddenly, he leaped at her and gave her a big hug. "Both on *and* under the stage."

"How's you-know-who?" Payton asked him.

"Safe and happy in my sleeve." Mason pointed to his arm. "Thank you for saving him."

"No problem," Payton said. "I *am* a *good* witch, remember?"

"And so am I," I said, laughing. "Although that part I'd rather *not* remember. Payton, you really were fabulous up there."

"Yeah, Payton, you totally rocked that bubble," Nick said, coming back, with Jason trotting behind him.

Nick was smiling at Payton. Hmm. It was kind of the way Ox used to look at me.

Nick and Payton? Payton and Nick? Hmm.

Suddenly, Mason looked suspiciously at Nick. I realized I wasn't the only one to notice that possibility. Mason moved so he was between Nick and Payton.

"Payton," Mason said. "I think you really rocked that bubble, too."

"Um, thanks," Payton said.

"Yeah, that was excellent," Nick said.

"Yeah, well, I think it was even excellenter!" Mason said louder. "I think it was excellent times two! Which is twice as much as you! See, Emma? I know my math!"

"Excuse us." I took Mason by the arm and half-dragged him off to the side. "Mason, what's up?"

"Nick!" he said indignantly. "Nick is trying to steal my woman."

I bit my lip to stop myself from smiling.

"You really like Payton?" I asked him.

"Duh! She's like my twin superwoman," he said. "She saved my gecko. And she let me make fart sound effects. She's perfect."

He got a faraway look in his eyes.

"Mason, I'm sure Payton thinks you're great," I said, trying to let him down gently.

"Really?" His eyes lit up.

"But *not* like that!" I hurriedly said. "You're four years younger than she is, Mason. That's just too young."

"Are you sure?" Mason looked disappointed.

"Yes. But, um, maybe when you're older," I said. "For example, when you're twenty-two, Payton will be twenty-six. That could work."

"Hey, that gives me an idea," Mason said. "I can marry Payton and you can marry Jason! You're both geniuses, so it's perfect."

Ack! Ick! Squick! I shook my head to clear that thought.

"I guess thinking Payton might like me was kinda dumb," Mason said. "I know, I'm the dumb twin."

"That's not true," I said firmly. "You just have a different kind of smarts than your brother. Like how you noticed Nick has a crush on Payton. Even Payton hadn't noticed that! That's called 'interpersonal smarts.'"

"Hmm," Mason said. "Well, Nick is okay for a second choice. He did show me the special effects."

I smiled at Mason. He was turning out to be an okay kid.

"I thought of another kind of smarts I have, too," Mason

said. "What's it called if you know how to make money?"

"Hmm, financial smarts?" I replied.

"Give me a dollar, and I won't tell my mom how you and Payton switched places tonight even though it's against the rules."

"That's not financial smarts, that's blackmail!" I said. "Besides, it's because of your gecko that we did it in the first place!"

Mason just smiled. Ergh. I take it back. He was not an okay kid. *Grrr.* I put my hand in my pocket and pulled out a dollar.

"Blackmail is not something to be proud of," I grumbled.

"I know, but I'm thirsty," he said. "I need the juice machine."

Jason came running up to us as I handed it over.

"Give me a buck, too, or I'll tell my mother you paid Mason off for . . . something," Jason said.

"See, Jason's got the blackmail smarts, too," Mason said. "We're identical like that."

"And here comes our mom and dad! Quick, Emma, a dollar gets you our 'perfect angel' act," Jason said. "Right, Mason?"

I sighed and pulled out another one.

"Oh, yeah, what I really came over for was to remind you to give Payton the envelope from my mother," Jason said.

"Oh!" I reached into my left hoodie pocket and pulled out the envelope for my sister.

"Bye, Emma!" Mason said, holding his father's hand.

"Thank you, Emma," Jason said, holding his mother's hand.

"Emma's cool," I heard one twin say.

"Not cool, exactly," the other disagreed. "But not bad for a math tutor."

I smiled. And finally they were gone. I should have felt relieved or peaceful or something. I looked down at my mathletes champion T-shirt. Even that didn't work. I wasn't cheered up. I felt kind of numb.

I stood in the entrance foyer of our school. It was empty except for a few people still lingering after the play. I stared at the GO, GECKOS! banner on the wall. I read the school rules poster. And then, the person I'd tried so hard to not think about came into my brain. Ox. Ox Ox Ox Ox Ox.

I started chewing on my hair.

Had I really meant what I'd said about balancing studying and hobbies *and* a social life? I did. So did that mean there was room for . . . Ox?

I pulled my cell phone out of the right pocket of my hoodie. I quickly typed in a text before I could change my mind or lose my nerve.

talk soon? :O

I pressed send. He probably wouldn't respond for a while. Maybe he'd met a new girl at Swirly's—a pretty mathlete from

one of the other schools. Maybe he'd never text me back. I'd basically blown him off. Why would he even want to talk to me?

I sighed and reread my text:

talk soon? :O

"Is now soon enough?"

I yelped (really, it did sound like "yelp"), and turned around
to see Ox. Live, in person.

"What are you doing here?" I asked, flustered.

"My neighbor Sam was one of the Munchkins," Ox said.
"My dad's waiting out in the truck. We're giving him a ride."

"A Munchkin?" I said. "Boy, his knees must be hurting."
*Great, Emma, brilliant conversationalist, talking about his neigh-
bor's knees.*

"Actually, I lent him my kneepads from football." Ox
laughed.

"Oh," I said. "Smart."

"What did you want to talk about?" Ox held up his cell
phone.

I hadn't had time to plan and organize my discussion with
Ox. I didn't even have an opening line prepared. What should
I say?

*Ox, you look so handsome. Ox, please like-like me again. Go,
Geckos.*

Nothing in my head sounded right. So. I turned off my
logic-brain and tried to say what I felt.

"Ox, I'm sorry," I said. That was a good start. "I thought I couldn't . . . *shouldn't* do anything except study for competitions, but I was wrong. I'd like for us to be friends, but if you don't want to be I'll understand. I just wanted you to know."

Ox looked up. He looked down. He crossed his arms and uncrossed them.

"Emma," Ox said. "I'm glad you took the time to figure out what you can handle. I'm really happy that you won mathletes and I'm really, really happy you want to be friends again. But there's a problem."

I knew it. I blew it.

"The problem is I want to be *more* than just friends," Ox said, his words rushing out faster. "But my dad is totally old-school, and I'm not allowed to date until I'm in high school."

"You—you want to *date* me?" I squeaked.

"Well, yeah." Ox looked right at me. "I'd be so lucky to have a girlfriend like you—funny, pretty, and smart."

Did he say "pretty"? *And* "girlfriend"? ? ? ? ?

"Oh, I'd be lucky to have a boyfriend like you," I stammered. "I mean, if you were allowed to date. Which is reasonable that you're not, considering you have football and mathletes and besides, we're only twelve." I was babbling.

"Thirteen," Ox said. "I'm actually thirteen."

"That's why you're so much more mature than I am," I blurted.

Ox looked at me. I looked at him. Then we both cracked up. It wasn't that funny. I was just feeling happy.

"Except I'm not allowed to date," Ox reminded me.

"That's okay," I assured him, "I don't think I'm ready for a boyfriend yet. But if I were, it would definitely be you."

"Well, okay then," Ox said, grinning. His cell phone buzzed. "It's my dad. No, Dad, Sam hasn't come out yet. I'm just talking to Emma."

Ox's voice got quieter.

"Yes, *that* Emma," he said into the phone.

That Emma? Ox's father knew who I was? Maybe just because I won mathletes. That must be it.

Ox turned to talk to me. "My dad wants to know if you want to go for pizza with our family sometime."

"Really?" Pizza with his family? Being out in public with Ox? Me? Ox and me?

"I'll have to ask my parents," I said, trying to sound calm. "But I'm sure they'll say *yes*."

"Uh-huh," Ox said back into the phone. "Yeah, bye." He put his phone back in his pocket and smiled.

I smiled.

Er—now what?

"Did you know that in Japan they put squid on their pizzas?" I asked. Arrgh . . . Why did inane trivia always pop out when I didn't know what else to say?

"I prefer mushrooms and peppers," Ox said.

"Those are my favorite toppings, too!" I exclaimed.

"Did you know in Brazil they like peas on their pizza?" Ox asked me.

And for the next two minutes we discussed pizza, math-letes, football, and endangered animals . . . until Ox's neighbor Sam came out (walking on his feet).

"Oh!" I remembered him. "You were the Munchkin with the Geckos cap." Oops. I'd seen that onstage when I was Glinda.

"Wow, you have good vision," Munchkin Sam said. "C'mon, Ox, we gotta go."

Ox winked at me.

I smiled at him.

"Call you later?" he asked me.

"Okay," I said to him.

And after he and Sam had left, I went, *"Eeeeeeeeeeeeeeee!"* and did a happy dance, not caring if anyone saw me. Because I could have academics *and* Quinn *and* Ox. All different, all amazing, and all just right for me, Emma Mills.

Payton

Twenty-five

GRAND FINALE

Bzzzt! Bzzzt!

I heard my cell phone buzz in my tote bag across from the dressing area. I'd check my text in a minute. I wanted to stop and let what just happened sink in.

This amazing moment where I had just gone onstage and played Glinda in the school play!

In a beautiful pink dress! And I'd remembered (almost) all the lines! I kind of felt like Cinderella after the ball as I took off the dress and hung it on the hanger. It was time to go back to reality.

Bzzzt! Bzzzt!

I pulled my cell out of my bag and read the text from Emma.

ox!!

 216

Ox! Oh my gosh! That must mean she talked to Ox! They made up! Maybe even more than made up! Maybe they were dating! I wondered if they were going out on a date even now.

I couldn't wait to congratulate her. Emma + Ox. Maybe someday they'd even get married. It was all so romantic.

The Mills twins were having an exciting day.

I bumped into Emma as soon as I left the dressing room. She had a goofy grin on her face. But before I had a chance to talk to her, a girl came up to us and stuck a microphone in Emma's face.

"Hi!" she said. "I'm Kendra, reporting for a special VOGS news story. May I interview you about the excitement?"

Oh my gosh! Big news traveled fast!

"You want to interview her about her new boyfriend for VOGS?" I squealed.

"Boyfriend?" Both Emma and the VOGS reporter asked and looked at me like I was crazy.

"Excuse us!" Emma half-dragged me off to the side. "Payton, what are you talking about?"

"She wants to interview you about your new romance!" I said. "You and Ox!"

"What are you talking about?" Emma asked. "She wants to interview me about winning *mathletes!*"

Oops.

"Oh," I said. "Um. Sorry. I got your text and got all excited about you and Ox being boyfriend and girlfriend."

"We're not. Ox isn't allowed to date," Emma said. Then she grinned. "But he did ask me to go out for pizza with his family!"

"Awww!" I said.

"Okay, that VOGS reporter is waiting for me," Emma said. "I need to refocus and talk about my astonishing mathletes win."

"Go, Emma!" I said, and followed her back to the VOGS reporter.

"So, who's your new boyfriend?" Kendra asked. "Not for official reports, just 'cause I like gossip."

"There's no new boyfriend," Emma said. "So let's move on to the official report."

"Okay, I'll stick with my story." Kendra sighed and switched on her video camera. "I'm here with the Mills twins after *The Wizard of Oz* play. So, how does it feel to have substituted for someone else and pulled it off so well?"

Wait, what? Oh, no. Were we being busted on live camera *again*? Did she know Emma had "substituted" for me onstage?

Emma and I gave each other worried glances.

"Um," Emma said. "Can you clarify the question?"

She was using her secret stalling tactic she used in her competitions, trying to have more time to think.

"Sure," Kendra said. "What was it like when you were told you were the last-minute substitute for Sydney after Sydney injured her foot?"

Oh!!! She was talking about *me* substituting!

I let out a sigh of relief at the same time Emma did.

"I think you're talking about my sister, Payton," Emma said, pointing to me.

"Oh, no, I mixed you guys up, Emma! I thought you were Payton!" Kendra giggled and turned to me. "Sorry!"

Okay! I was being interviewed. I smiled and prepared to answer the question.

"Take two!" Kendra said. "So, Payton, what was it like when you were told you were the last-minute substitute for the actress playing Glinda after she injured her foot?"

"Of course I didn't want anyone to get hurt," I said. "But I think everyone in the cast and crew did a great job rallying together and putting on a great show."

"And . . . cut!" Kendra said, turning off the camera. "Thanks. It will be on VOGS next week. And sorry again about mixing you guys up."

"That's okay," I said. "It happens all the time. Just remember, I'm the taller twin. And my eyes are a teeny bit greener."

"And I have a faint freckle on my cheek," Emma said. "And my hair is shinier."

"Hey," I protested.

"Remember, the gecko proved it," Emma said.

"Maybe when you actually *brush* it," I muttered. "Which is rare."

"Okay." Kendra laughed. "No fighting! I get it. I can tell who is who."

"Who is *whom*," Emma said to her. "Not who is *who*. Just FYI."

"Emma." I shot her a look.

"What?" Emma said. "People want to know they are making grammatical errors. And that gives me a great idea! VOGS is seen by the whole school. Kendra, can you turn on your camera so I can give a minilesson on *who* versus *whom*? Everyone keeps making that mistake."

No. No. NO!

"Look, there's the star of *Wizard of Oz!*" I said loudly, and pointed to Tess. "Kendra, did you interview Tess yet?"

"Not yet! Where is she?" Kendra asked, looking relieved to get away from us.

"Let Tess get interviewed," I hissed to Emma. Thankfully, she nodded.

Kendra turned her camera on Tess. "Tess, how was it playing Dorothy?"

"It was amazing!" Tess said, beaming. "Everyone was so great! Like Payton, jumping in at the last minute without even rehearsing with us! That was awesome!"

Now I was beaming.

"What a great day!" Tess said. "Did you know Emma won her mathletes today, too?"

Now Emma was beaming. We all shared a happy moment of complimenting each other. And as if our happy moment couldn't get any better, Reilly walked up to us. He'd scrubbed off his Scarecrow makeup and his hair was all messed up from wearing the straw hat.

Ahhh! Reilly! So cute! I sighed. So did Tess. And Kendra.

And Emma! I was not alone in my appreciation of his cuteness.

"Don't you want to interview The Scarecrow?" Reilly asked the VOGS reporter.

"Sure!" She giggled, blushing. She turned the camera on him. "Congratulations on your play!"

"Thanks," he said. "I was good, huh? Did you see the part where I threw the apple back at the tree? Pretty funny, huh? And how about when I said . . ."

We watched as Reilly talked about himself for a while.

"He could have mentioned you guys," Emma whispered to me.

Okay, true. He was a lot cuter when he didn't speak.

"VOGS!" A loud voice made us all jump. It was Mrs. Burkle. "Are you getting good coverage for VOGS?"

Kendra nodded.

"Excellent!" she said. "Did you interview Payton? She has marvelous stage presence on camera as well. Payton, when are you joining us on VOGS again?"

Everyone looked at me.

"Um, I can't do any after-schools until my school service is over," I said, embarrassed.

"What? Who makes these rules?" Burkle demanded.

"Maybe I should be on VOGS," Reilly said. "The camera loves me."

"Oh, that reminds me!" Emma said to me, while Reilly was talking about himself. "I have something for you from Counselor Case. I have one, too."

She pulled out an envelope and handed it to me. I opened it up as she started opening hers.

To: Payton
From: Counselor Case
You have completed your school service by going above and beyond the call of duty this evening. Congratulations! Your service is finished.

"Ahhhh!" I said. "I'm free! I'm done with school service!"

"Yay!" Tess said. "You deserve it after all the hard work you did!"

"Fabulous!" Burkle said. "Report to VOGS next week. And, speaking of which, Kendra appears to have forgotten to interview someone integral to this show. Namely the director, me."

She hustled off for her turn on camera.

"Yay!" I said to Emma. "No school service. We're free!"

"No," Emma said, frowning. "*You* are free. I have to continue . . ."

"Counselor Case can't give you up, can she?" I asked her. "You're just too good at tutoring those twins."

"But wait!" Emma's face brightened as she read further. "She added she's going to pay me to tutor the boys. And I make my own hours. Looks like I have a job! I'll be able to buy the new scientific graphing calculator! *Squee!*"

"Did you just *squee* over a calculator?" I shook my head.

 222

"Hey, are you guys ready to go?" Nick asked. "I think people are heading over."

"Go where?" I asked.

"Cast party," Nick said. "You *are* going, right?"

"Oh, I didn't know about it," I said. "You know, since I wasn't part of the cast or anything until tonight."

"Oh, you were on the list," Tess said. "Nick put you down as his guest weeks ago. Didn't you, Nick?"

"Er . . ." Nick looked uncomfortable. "Well, since Payton had helped under the stage she deserved to go to the cast party."

"Hmm," Tess said. "And that's the only reason?"

Nick blushed. Wait a minute. Oh! OH!

"Glar," I said. *Glar?* What was "glar"? Why did I say *glar?*

Emma walked back over to us.

"Sorry, I need to borrow Payton for a minute," Emma said.

"Okay," Nick said. "If I can have her back for the cast party."

Oh!

Emma half-dragged me to the side of the stage.

"I thought you needed a minute to pull yourself together," Emma said. "You were turning purple."

"Me?" I asked. "*You're* the one who turns purple when she talks to boys."

"You're apparently getting us mixed up right now," she said. "You're purple. Maybe you only turn purple when you talk to boys you *like*."

"Agh," I said, and fanned my face. Nick? I liked Nick? Nick likes me?!

"What a crazy night," Emma said. "It was quite impressive we pulled that off. Although, we should probably promise not to trade places *or* substitute for each other again," Emma said. "Shouldn't we?"

"I don't know," I said. "I think having two Paytons—and zero Emmas—could be a good thing. Two Paytons! No Emmas!"

"Hey!" Emma said. "You mean two Emmas and zero Paytons."

"Two Paytons!" I said, laughing. "Two twins who have 'stage presence' and also are one inch taller," I added.

"Two twins with the shinier hair *and* exceptional math abilities," Emma countered.

"Two PooPas and no MeeMas," I added.

"Two Poopys," Emma said. "Poopy."

"Wow, genius response from the genius Emma." I laughed. "Poopy?"

"Your nickname," Emma said. "Remember? You told me they were calling you Poopy?"

"I don't remember that," I pretended. "I think the great AcadEmma just likes saying Poopy."

"Poopy," Emma said. "Poopy. You're a poopyhead."

"You've been hanging out with Mason and Jason too long," I said.

"Doofus," Emma replied, laughing.

"Are you two talking in your secret twin language again?" Tess came up to us, smiling.

"No, Emma's just losing it," I said.

"If Emma can keep it together, we're all leaving for the cast party," Tess told us. "Payton, Nick offered you a ride."

I turned red. Okay, maybe a pale shade of purple.

"So, when you two both have boyfriends, will you switch places on them?" Tess asked.

Emma and I looked at each other.

"I'm not going to have a boyfriend for a long time," Emma said. "At least officially. *Ahem*. So I'm going to focus on my true interest. Academics. And fashion websites. And, well, I do need some new shoes for the winter, so maybe a little shopping may have to be fit in. But not boyfriends."

"And Payton can focus on her interests!" Tess said. "Auditioning for the next play! Being part of VOGS! Hanging out with me!"

"And boys," both Emma and I said at the same time.

"Twinx!" we both shouted and then laughed.

"Buy me a soda," I said to Emma.

"Tess will have to do it for me," Emma said. "At the cast party. You guys have fun!"

"Oh, you're coming to the cast party, too, Emma," Tess said.

"I am?" Emma asked her.

"Yeah. Officially, as my guest," Tess said. "But, unofficially, well, it's for everyone who was in the play, right?"

And she looked at Emma. And she looked at me.

"Emma, you have a faint freckle on your cheek," Tess said. And then she winked. "And Dorothy noticed Glinda did, too, at first . . ."

Busted. She totally knew we'd switched places onstage!

"Well," Emma stammered. "There were emergency circumstances to our situation."

"And," I sputtered, "it's not exactly like we were *trading* places. More like . . . substituting. And we're done with that. We're never doing it again!"

As Tess walked in front of us, laughing, I held out my pinky to Emma for a pinky swear.

Emma held out her pinky, too. But, we didn't link pinkies. No twinky swears on that one. Because stuff happens. And I guess you should never say "never"!

Acknowledgments

Double thanks to:
The family: Greg Roy, Adam Roy, Dave DeVillers, Quinn DeVillers, and Jack DeVillers.

The Simon & Schuster crew: Bethany Buck, Fiona Simpson, Mara Anastas, Alyson Heller, Paul Crichton, Andrea Kempfer, Lucille Rettino, Bess Braswell, Venessa Williams, Karin Paprocki, Katherine Devendorf, and Kathy Lovisolo.

The agents: Mel Berger and William Morris Endeavor Agency; Alyssa Eisner Henkin, and Trident Media Group.

And: Mark McVeigh, Lauren Heller Whitney, Anna DeRoy, Anne Elisa Schaeffer, Daphne Chan, Jen Corrigan, Crandall Public Library, and Columbus Metropolitan Library.

And: Thanks to Paige Pooler, our illustrator. Paige Pooler rocks!